THE GOLDEN DUCK

Vivienne Wayman

St. Martin's Press
New York

Library of Congress Cataloging-in-Publication Data
Wayman, Vivienne.
    The golden duck / Vivienne Wayman.
       p.   cm.
    "A Thomas Dunne book."
    ISBN 0-312-05868-3
    I. Title.
  PR6073.A935G6   1991
  823'.914—dc20   90-21950
                                                            CIP

First published in Great Britain by Macmillan London Limited.

First U.S. Edition: May 1991
10 9 8 7 6 5 4 3 2 1

For Nin

PART ONE

1

It was the hottest day of the year. The mallards sat about in indolent heaps on the grass beside the narrow river that ran swiftly under the road to the sea. A solitary duck moved on the water, an elegant duck that differed from the rest because of its gold and white and coffee-coloured feathers. Only the small violet-blue patch on either wing indicated its relationship to the rest of the mallards.

It turned to swim under the road-bridge into shadows that transformed its plumage to moth-brown. A small buttress had been erected at some time to strengthen the brickwork at the sea end of the bridge, where decomposing vegetation and twigs and other rubbish that drifted in the current had become trapped. Today there was more than usual. The duck paddled towards it.

Something bulky had caught in the angle of the bricks. It rocked, half-submerged, under matted weed and sticks, like a waterlogged sack. The floating debris was pushed aside as the object rose up. Hair lay in strands, black with wetness, over the skin of the head, which knocked gently against the wall. A white bloated hand lifted from the water and sank. Weed moved across to close the gap.

The duck stretched forward to pull at a weed before it turned and swam back into the sunlight with fronds of green clinging to its shiny wet bill.

2

At two o'clock in the afternoon Rosemary Lawrence was lying in the bath to cool herself down. Outside the open window everything was silent in the stifling heat. She would have preferred to have driven to the beach at Brancaster for a swim but Peter had the car and her conscience persuaded her that it would be an imposition to ask her friend Charlotte. Not that she would have minded. One could nearly always swim at Brancaster, unlike the other local stretches of sand, where Nick said the sea ran over the edge of the world when the tide was out. Rosemary's son Nick was in Paris doing a course on art appreciation and improving his accent at the same time, she hoped. It was costing enough.

Lying back in the bath she could see the familiar crack winding across the ceiling. She was convinced it was getting longer. The house was really too large for them, despite the fact that it was just the wing of the original Victorian building, the only part to survive when the rest was demolished by fire before the war. The place was steadily going downhill and it showed, unlike Charlotte's Georgian house, where the slow decline gave it the dignity of an impoverished aristocrat. Charlotte never bothered about repairs.

Rosemary lifted one foot to rest it on the pitted tap. Marsh House demanded constant attention. Tiles descended, pointing crumbled from the chimneys, birds insulated the loft with nests, blocked gutters hung dangerously and rotting window-frames sloughed off paint like skin from a burnt sun-worshipper. Even indoors slugs emerged from crevices at night, leaving glistening trails on the carpets. Peter spent all his weekends happily making good.

The lodge that stood at the entrance to the drive, was a legacy from the old house. New tenants had moved in last week, inspiring Rosemary to paint the blistering front door white in their honour. She had taken Kenneth Weaver and his wife and their large golden retriever over the small cottage a few days previously. He was tall and bearded with a low voice like Jeremy Iron's. His wife, apparently called Cat, was short and bossy, and wore an enormous pair of spectacles pushed up into her dark hair like two red-rimmed saucers. She had lowered them once with equally red, long fingernails to gaze out of the upstairs window, complaining that the trees in the garden obscured the view. Peter had removed a few, Rosemary told her, adding that perhaps her husband would cut down one or two more if she asked him, although she had no intention of doing so.

Cat had replaced her glasses before she produced a tape-measure from her pocket which she and Kenneth stretched along the hall between the doors, vertically and horizontally, calling out measurements to each other. Finally they agreed that there was enough room after commenting that wasn't it a good thing the stairs rose into the wall without constricting the space. Rosemary watched all this in perplexed amusement.

'There's my Steinway, you see,' said Cat, winding the tape-measure into a hard roll. 'We'll have to get it through the hall.'

'I hope we won't be noisy neighbours,' said Kenneth. 'As we're isolated here, practising shouldn't be a problem.'

Cat said that they wanted to come immediately, before she disappeared to work in Europe for a few weeks. So they had moved in with the dog and the grand piano.

Rosemary twisted the soap in her hands and rubbed the bubbles down one arm. She hoped the Weavers appreciated the new cooker in the kitchen as well as the shiny front door, both financed by Rosemary after the sale of three paintings.

She was still experiencing that slightly twitchy feeling that came over her when things had not gone right. The watercolour she had attempted early that morning on the salt-marsh had acquired a crude look, all the luminosity in the sky lost under a wash that had dried unsuitably heavy. There was nothing she could do about it. Oils could be scraped down and repainted – watercolours were permanent. All the same, she preferred watercolour because it was so immediate. She would ditch today's work and begin afresh tomorrow.

The telephone rang. It was only the thought that it might be Emma or Nick that made her step, one dripping foot after another, out of the water. She wound a towel under her arms as she ran, pressing a trail of wet footprints into the landing carpet.

When she lifted the receiver the hoarse smoker's voice of Betty Tiller spoke from the village shop.

'Rosey love, Betty here.'

'Hello, Betty.' The reply was flat with disappointment. 'What can I do for you?'

'Listen, I must be brief because I've got a shop full of customers. I've got this girl here. She's whacked, poor kid. She wants one of your beds for the night.'

'But Betty, we don't let rooms any more. I thought you knew.'

'Hang on, love. Of course I know. She's a friend of your Emma's. From Dublin. They met on that trip she did.'

'Dublin!'

'Right. I told her your Emma was cavorting in the Med somewhere and she said what a pity as it's Emma she's come to see. Emma gave her your address and said she'd be welcome any time.'

'I see.' Rosemary had suffered the consequences of her daughter's generous invitations before.

Betty was droning on. 'Fortunately she called at the shop and of course I was able to tell her where you lived.'

'Thanks.'

The voice on the phone became distant. 'What did you say your name was, darling?' It boomed again, gathering speed. 'Yes, it's Kate. Look, Rosey, I must get back to the counter

12

before they start a riot. I'll send her round. Thought I'd put you in the picture first.'

'Could you give me half an hour?' said Rosemary. 'I've just got out of the bath.'

'Will do. I'll delay her with an ice-lolly.'

Rosemary sighed. Emma was always doing this. By now she should have got used to bulging sleeping-bags that had not been there when she went to bed, littering the floor of the sitting room the following day. Nick was as bad.

'Morning everybody,' Rosemary had schooled herself to say. 'Tea or coffee?'

'Well, if you live by the sea, what do you expect?' she muttered, leaving damp patches on the quilt when she got up.

She had not really expected Emma or Nick to phone, not until they needed to be collected from somewhere.

It was five years since she had let rooms and then only a double and a single to get them through a sticky financial period. It had not been worth the hassle. For one thing Rosemary had missed the freedom of being able to go out early on to the salt-marsh when the light had that special quality and the shadows were long. Then, quite by chance, she had discovered a gallery that would show her paintings, along with others, and the money she received when they were sold became a pleasanter way of adding to their income.

This Kate would have to sleep in Emma's room because Rosemary had taken over the large spare room as a studio and the other one had become a dump so that now the door would not fully open because of the clutter wedged inside.

Emma was in her last year at school in Lynn. She had gone with a friend on one of those student holidays under canvas that boasted midnight barbecues on foreign beaches but never mentioned the long drives through the night when one of the party was allocated to talk to the driver to keep him awake. The thought of it kept Rosemary awake.

She dressed and flung up the window in Emma's room. It was like an oven. She emptied one of the drawers into a suitcase and opened the wardrobe door where the confined sleeve of Emma's jingle-jacket slid out: Peter had christened it thus because of its many gold chains. The material was peach cotton embellished in the worst possible taste, Nick had remarked scornfully. Swirls of crusty white paint had been added and gold chains, looped and dangled, attached to the fabric with huge plastic gems. Even Emma had decided it was too magnificent to cart around Europe. She had admitted to no one what she had paid for it. How they spent their own money had always been the children's business.

Rosemary pushed the sleeve back and closed the door cautiously. Emma's friend would have to manage with a couple of hangers behind the door. There was no need for fresh sheets as they were already clean awaiting Emma's return. Dusting her collection of grotesque little animals was time-consuming. After half-a-dozen had been lifted and replaced, Rosemary lowered her mouth to the level of the chest and blew gently. An elephant the size of a large beetle, banging a drum, toppled and disappeared over the edge. As she examined it for damage the doorbell rang. She plucked a yellow sock from the carpet and, thrusting it into her pocket, ran downstairs.

The girl standing on the step had her back to Rosemary. She was short, little more than five feet, and Rosemary's first impression was of hair, a great cascade of it, the colour of wet sand, falling smooth and heavy to a tightly belted waist. Below it her floral skirt, home-made Rosemary guessed by the puckered seams, reached nearly to her feet which were bare and grubby. Beside her stood a faded holdall, fastened with a belt because the open zip appeared to have broken. Her discarded sandals were balanced on top. From behind she could have been fourteen years old, but when she turned her shape above and below the small waist was what Peter would describe as satisfactorily rounded. She wore a limp T-shirt that had the words 'Dublin's Bubblin'' printed across the front.

The girl studied Rosemary with eyes the colour of spring

14

leaves. A short upper lip gave her mouth a full, square look in a face that was attractively plump. She could have been eighteen or much older.

'Hello,' said Rosemary. 'You must be Kate.'

The girl nodded. Perspiration beaded her forehead.

'Oh, you're hot,' said Rosemary. 'Your poor feet. Aren't they sore?'

'No.' Kate's voice was high.

'Come on in. Emma told me all about you.' This was untrue but it sounded welcoming. 'Sorry she's not here but she's in Greece or Turkey or somewhere.'

'Yes, I know that.' With a hand that still bore the marks of the handle across the palm, Kate lifted the holdall.

'I've given you Emma's room,' said Rosemary over her shoulder, as they climbed the stairs. In the bedroom Kate walked straight to the window.

'The sea. That's great.' Her mouth thinned to a slow, wide smile.

'Yes. My husband cleared a gap in the trees so that we would have that view. You can see the old harbour. It's only used for small boats now as it's silted up. When this house was built trees were planted all round to form a windbreak.'

'I like private places.' Kate flung her holdall on to the patchwork quilt that Rosemary had sewn by hand for Emma's tenth birthday. Near the pillow the legs of her bald teddy bear jolted at the bump.

Kate was shown the empty drawers and the brass hook behind the door as Rosemary apologised for the full wardrobe. A shelf on the wall beside the bed was equally crowded, with books lying flat and others stacked upright. Kate showed interest.

'Do you like reading, Kate?'

'Yes. Passionate love-stories that have happy endings.' She laughed.

There were none of those in Emma's collection as far as Rosemary knew.

15

Kate raised her eyes to look at a Klimt poster on the wall. 'That's a funny old picture. Are they making love, those two?'

'Well, yes. I think so.'

'It's all squiggles.'

'The bathroom's at the end of the passage if you'd like a shower.'

'I'll wash my hair,' said Kate, stroking a lopsided pottery hedgehog.

'That's one of Emma's efforts from her junior school,' said Rosemary. 'You'll find a hairdrier in the bathroom cabinet. Come down as soon as you're ready.'

The sun shone hotly down. Charlotte Franklin, her skin gleaming with perspiration and oil, was browning uncomfortably in the garden. She turned her head to rest it on her plump, folded arms so that she faced the oak growing beside the narrow river that ran out of her garden and under the road bridge. Her son, Colin, had seen a tawny owl roosting in the tree. If it were there now it was inconspicuous in the massed foliage.

The dark shadow under the oak looked tempting. A small winged insect kept landing on her leg, tickling through the fine hairs. She kicked it away, thinking that lying in the sun was an absurd way of spending the time but she must persevere to tan her skin so that she could discard the dark tights she wore to make her heavy legs appear slimmer.

The insect returned. It wasn't any good. She would have to go indoors. As she climbed to her feet she noticed that the soil on the rose-bed was invisible under a healthy layer of groundsel. She must try to persuade Colin to tug the stuff out even if it meant offering a small bribe of cash. He was a disaster at weeding as he slaughtered both weeds and flowers indiscriminately but Charlotte imagined he couldn't do much damage to the rose-bushes. He would moan about the thorns, of course.

She pulled a long black floating shift over her black control swimsuit and ran to the shadow of the house where

16

the grass was cool under her feet. She went through the French windows into the living room and flopped on to a settee where the pattern of cream and orange flowers had blurred on the grubby cushions and the arms had rubbed to strings of thread at the edges. Ten years ago, when her husband was alive, the decorations in this room had been carried out with enthusiasm, but now the bamboo-coloured carpet was only bright under the furniture and the white paintwork had yellowed until it matched the emulsion on the walls.

Charlotte lived in the back of the house in a room that combined the original kitchen and morning room. The scullery had been converted into a kitchen that she had considered modern until she saw Vicky Barclay's sumptuous fitments. The drawing room and dining room that ran across the front of the house were only invaded once or twice a year. Then, Mrs Wolfe polished the damp bloom off the antique furniture while Charlotte wound and set the five chiming clocks that George had never allowed to run down and a fire was lit in each chilly grate.

Charlotte was bored but not depressingly so. She was always on the verge of getting round to things, it was just that no project excited her enough to spur her into action. She was about to reach for a cigarette when she noticed the cat's saucer on the floor. Mr Puss had left the remains of some evil-smelling fish clinging to it and pieces had fallen on to the carpet where a large fly hovered noisily before it settled. Charlotte hated flies. She got up to wave it away and transferred the pieces of dropped fish to the saucer with distaste. In the kitchen she scraped its contents into the pedal-bin and made herself a cup of coffee dropping in ice-cubes to cool it. Black coffee because she was dieting.

She sat down and lit a cigarette, enjoying the taste and the smell of the smoke. She didn't seem to be losing weight very fast. The rounded figure that had attracted her late husband was beginning to get out of hand. She was constantly concerned about it, dressing in loose black garments when she was desperate or, after a successful bout of dieting, in autumnal shades to complement her hair which had the patina of a newly fallen conker. It had been more distinctive before the colour became available to others from a bottle. At least she never had a tell-tale parting.

She had married George Franklin when he was forty-one and she was twenty. Now, twenty-three years later, George was dead and Charlotte continued to live in the house with their only son, Colin. George had left them well provided for, investing money for Colin's future as the boy was incapable of earning any of his own.

Charlotte's biggest asset was her charm. People called on Charlotte. They always came to the back of the house, often for no reason than to be first with a bit of gossip, but at other times for sympathy or a good unburdening moan. Her sherry-coloured eyes glowed as she listened with genuine concern. She welcomed anyone at any time, even if she was just on her way out, which meant she was invariably late for appointments, but with or without this excuse she was rarely punctual. People were never annoyed because they liked her.

Mr Puss jumped up behind Charlotte exhaling fishy breath and crept down one arm to her lap. A pointed ear flicked as the cat lowered itself, warm and plump, across her ample thighs. Its purr became as monotonous as a distant farm tractor.

Kate had come into the sitting room so silently that Rosemary, who was frowning over her sketching block, had not realised she was there.

Kate looked at the painting. 'That's really great,' she said.

Rosemary held it at arms' length. 'I don't know. I'm not satisfied with it.'

'Did you do it?'

Rosemary nodded.

'And all those gorgeous ones hanging in the hall?'

'Yes.'

'I wish I could paint like that.'

'I expect you're good at other things.'

Kate wandered towards the bookcase where there was a photograph of Emma smiling in the sun.

'That's Emma,' said Rosemary.

'I know,' said Kate. 'It's a good likeness.'

She sat down on the floor beside the open French windows where she could look out at the trees that encircled the garden. A swift screamed as it dived low over the grass.

'Sorry you missed Emma,' said Rosemary.

'When will she be back?' Kate tucked her feet under her flowery skirt.

'Not for ages. She only left last week. She might ring but we don't depend on it. My guess is that she'll just turn up,' said Rosemary. 'I'm glad you came anyway, Kate. I hope you won't find it too boring without her.'

Kate didn't reply.

'What did you say your surname was?'

'O'Dwyer.'

'How long have you been in England, Kate?'

'No time at all. I came over on the ferry to Holyhead and stopped off in London for a bit. Then I decided to visit Emma, so here I am now.'

'Did you come up by train?'

'I've no money to be wasting on trains. Sure, I hitched and walked from Hunstanton.'

'Walked! All that way!'

'And why not? It's healthy exercise so it is. I walk miles in the Wicklows.'

Rosemary began to think that her questions were becoming intrusive.

Kate stared into the garden. The thick wall of trees hung over last year's leaves which lay in a crisp beige carpet around the trunks.

'I love this place,' she said. 'It's so secluded.'

'That's one way of putting it.' Rosemary chuckled. 'Peter, my husband, is not a gardener. Consequently things are inclined to get out of hand. He grows excellent fruit though. I hope there'll be some raspberries for supper.'

Kate lifted her hand to catch the newly washed hair

behind her neck and drew it down through her fingers in a sweeping, sensual movement.

'That's a grand lawn,' she said. After a watering from last week's rain the grass had the rough look of a home-made rug, speckled white where the daisies grew.

'It needs cutting badly,' said Rosemary. 'A friend's son does it for us.'

'That would spoil it,' said Kate.

Rosemary did not add that having it cut was an extravagance but also a kindness that they did not feel they could give up.

'Someone's playing a piano,' said Kate. The heavy chords of a Beethoven sonata carried across the garden.

'One of the tenants at the lodge,' said Rosemary. 'She's a professional.'

Now that there were tenants living there she must definitely do something about the grass. She remembered that she had a pile of charity envelopes to distribute. If she pestered Charlotte she could leave a message for Colin about the grass-cutting without it being too pointed.

She told Kate that she was going out to use the blackmail of friendship to extract money from the villagers.

'Do you mind if I desert you for half an hour?'

Kate stood up with alacrity. 'Will I come with you?'

'Of course, if you'd like to. Come and meet a few people.'

3

The eyes of the peeking ducks watched old Ben Pearce, his shirtsleeves rolled up above his elbows, clipping the privet hedge in his small front garden. He lowered the shears to rest his aching arms and glanced at the rows of spinach and early cauliflowers that grew around him. They would need watering later on. Filling every part of the front and side of his garden, as well as the back, had become a habit when he had a family to feed, so much so that now it was impossible to leave any of the earth unproductive. Even when his children could have done with a bit of grass to play on he had considered it wasteful. This year, as usual, he would give one or two cauliflowers and a few leaves of spinach away before he dug in the rest and next year he would plant as much again.

Flowers were an extravagance. Even Pol's sweet peas had been that. Every spring she had criss-crossed the fence with twine and watched the flowers smother it in pink and white and purple. She had a passion for the scent. She would fill vases and jam-jars and put them everywhere in the cottage, ignoring the dropping petals which normally sent her cursing for the dust-pan and brush.

As Ben continued to snip at the hedge he realised that Pol had been dead for ten years. 'Ten years come September,' he muttered. 'Caw, don't time fly!'

He wondered if his daughter, Hilda, still lived in the village a couple of miles inland. He'd had a bust-up with her a few years back and he hadn't seen her since. That bastard of a husband of hers was to blame. Something to do with Pol's mother's clock which Hilda said she'd been

21

promised. Well, she hadn't got it, and the clock was still on his mantelpiece. It had a wooden case, oak he thought, carved, with a gold face and a broken chime. That didn't bother him, it kept good time, a nice old piece, worth quite a bit he reckoned. Hilda would get it when he was gone but until then she could whistle for it. Pity he couldn't leave it to the boy. Percy had been killed in a motorbike accident in Cambridge, just after the war.

He still missed Pol although she could be a bit of a tartar. Rows were a necessary way of life to her. She'd been one for a spotless house and sparkling the windows had been an obsession. She'd sit on the outside windowledge with her back to the sea and her varicosed legs folded into the bedroom, shouting complaints to him in the garden and orders to the kids inside. All the time she'd rub and rub at the glass using a scrunched-up page from the local paper. She got a better shine than with that pricey muck from the village shop, she'd always say, and what if her hands did get black from the print. They'd wash.

Now Ben's windows were washed by the intermittent rain. Life had changed so much he wondered sometimes if he had imagined some of it.

He lived in a cottage that was originally one in a terrace of three separate dwellings. As they had been built at right-angles to the road, his gable-end had the only window with a view of the sea, unless the occupants behind leaned dangerously from their bedroom windows. The other two cottages belonged to one couple now; they had been bought by a London architect who had gutted them to make one house. And his wife was determined to have Ben's cottage.

Ben and Pol had moved in soon after the First World War when Hilda was a baby and there he intended to stay until he was moved out feet first, despite the money the architect was offering. What would he do with it anyway?

The gold and white mallard rose from the grass and moved forward in a rolling waddle towards two people it had noticed walking along the road. The other ducks struggled up to follow. Ben saw that it was Rosemary Lawrence

22

and a young girl he didn't recognise. Rosemary clapped her hands sharply to disperse the ducks enough for the two of them to step off the road on to the grass in front of Ben's cottage. She introduced Kate.

Ben cupped a hand round one ear and poked his head forward like a tortoise to catch Rosemary's raised voice.

'Kate O'Dwyer,' she repeated. 'She's staying with us for a bit.'

Ben nodded. He was used to hearing part of a sentence and guessing at the rest with no comment, otherwise people kept repeating themselves. Mrs Lawrence was easier than most because she opened her mouth wide.

'Tidying up your privet, I see,' she said. 'Mind you, don't overdo it in this sun.'

Ben pointed the blades of his shears over one frail shoulder. 'That chap from London, he say to me, "You haven't cut your hedge," and I say "No, I ain't," and he say, "Let me have a go at it with my 'lectric cutter," and I say, "No, I won't." That Barclay chap think he own the place.'

Kate, who was admiring the ducks, glanced up as he spoke.

'I'm sure he meant it kindly,' said Rosemary.

'Caw, he only say it to butter me up. And that tarty woman of his!' Ben sent a twig of yellow privet flying from a bad-tempered chop of the shears. 'She smoke like a drain, yeah! They come down here weekends to make my life a misery. She want me out you know.'

Rosemary made sympathetic noises. To change the subject she asked if he had seen Colin Franklin about, as she wanted him to cut the grass.

'That Colin Franklin!' said Ben. 'Useless as a chocolate teapot!'

'He makes a good job of our lawn.' She was being loyal to Charlotte rather than Colin, who made a reasonable job of half the grass or even less. Someone else had to rake up the cuttings.

'Thick as a plank, that one. I could do better at my age.' Ben gave Kate a sharp nod. 'I'm ninety year old you know!' He was eighty-eight.

Kate didn't say she would never have guessed it. She was looking at one persistent duck that had lifted its bill vertically towards her hand. It was different from the rest. She noticed its pale coffee back-feathers, gold edged with dark centres, that became larger and darker as they grew nearer the tail. It moved one webbed foot and stood on her toes.

'You should be inside, Ben, taking it easy,' said Rosemary, loudly. 'It's too hot for cutting hedges.'

'That Colin Franklin. He gawp at me through my hawthorn hedge.'

Rosemary could have pointed out that it was Colin's hedge, too, as his garden was on the other side, but all she said was, 'He watches birds. I expect there's a nest in there.'

Ben spat. 'I'll soon have that out with a broom-handle.'

'Oh, yes!' said Rosemary. 'I know someone who cooked potato peelings for the ducks last winter.'

'Who's that then?' Ben winked at Kate's expressionless face. 'Good as people, ducks are. Better!'

'You old shocker,' Rosemary murmured, adding loudly, 'You're due for a visit to Dr Macey's soon. I'll run you down there.'

'That Mr Petherbridge usually do it. I got pills enough to overflow a barrel. They don't do no good. Cough, cough, cough, all night I do.'

'But you must take the ones for your heart. Be sensible now.'

'Sensible! Course I am. Always have been.'

The golden mallard went down the bank in a dusty rush.

'Fancy a few raspberries?' said Rosemary.

'Rattle with pills, I do.' He wiped his damp face and blew his nose on a grey handkerchief.

Rosemary waited for the blast to subside. 'Like some raspberries, Ben?'

'Wouldn't mind, missus. Ta, one or two would be a rare treat.'

Kate, who had been watching the rings of water expand

round the duck, said quickly, 'Will I be bringing the raspberries along for you then?'

'Thank you, Kate,' said Rosemary, answering for Ben.

They left him and stopped at the road bridge that spanned
the narrow river to look down into the water. They could
hear clods of earth thudding on to the ground from over
the hedge and the sound of Ben's voice abusing Colin who
was a mile away watching a marsh harrier perched on a
dead tree.

Kate leaned over the stone parapet.

'It's deeper than you think,' said Rosemary.

In the water four ducks tugged at the submerged reeds.
They were an odd collection. Rosemary explained that
last year one of the mallard drakes had mated with a
white domestic duck which had since disappeared. Their
offspring had inherited mixed plumage, ranging from nearly
all white to the typical tawny colour of a female. Each bore
the violet-blue wing patch of a mallard.

Kate recognised the duck that had stood on her toes.
'That's a beautiful bird, now.'

'Dilly calls her Blondie,' said Rosemary. 'Dilly's another
octogenarian. What a character! Wait till you meet her!'

Behind a wall that had a break in it to let the river flow
through, a plank bridge, with a flimsy hand-rail, linked the
strip of grass beside Ben's hawthorn hedge and a garden.
A giant oak cast its shadow over clumps of red campion
growing on the banks of the river.

'Would that be where Colin lives?' asked Kate.

'Yes. And his mother. You'll like her. Let's go and
wave our envelopes at her, shall we?'

They passed through an open gate badly in need of a fresh
coat of paint. Trees and bushes obscured part of the square,
decaying house that stood on the curve of a pot-holed drive.
In the centre an elegant front door with a fanlight had the
additional shelter of a portico resting on two Ionic pillars.
Blown leaves banked up inside the porch, pressing against
the door. Urns of straggly geraniums on the step barred the
entrance. Four well-proportioned sash windows let light into

the front rooms which, like the door, were rarely opened.

Rosemary and Kate walked round to the back of the house to find Charlotte.

A few hours later Peter Lawrence was in his garden removing the bricks and skewers that held down the rudimentary bird deterrent he had erected to protect his raspberries. While he was rolling the net back to get at the fruit he became aware of Kate, who was watching him through her open bedroom window.

'Come on down, why don't you,' he called. 'It's lovely out here.'

She came and stood half in the bushes pulling the ripe fruit into her palm before she trickled each handful into the bowl on the ground. The silence between them was relaxed and friendly.

'Look, we're going to this party tomorrow,' said Peter. 'A couple of weekenders from London are giving it. A very informal affair. Why don't you come along?'

'I haven't been invited.'

'That doesn't matter.'

Kate still seemed doubtful. 'I'll think about it.'

'To tell the truth I always feel a bit inadequate myself in the company of these sophisticated urban types.' Peter realised that this confession would make her all the more reluctant to go. 'Oh, come on. We'll keep each other company.'

She bent to pick up a large raspberry that had fallen under a bush.

'Anyway, I haven't got a frock to wear.'

'You look very nice as you are.'

After supper she took a bowl of raspberries to Ben. When she returned she told Peter that she would go with them to the party.

'That Kate's a sweet kid,' he said to Rosemary as they were getting ready for bed.

4

As the holly-red Porsche drove on to the grassy area in front of Ben's cottage his angry eyes rose above the twigs of the partly cropped privet. He swore. It was her – it was that grasping bitch next door and look where she'd parked her ugly great motor, just where it blocked his view.

Ben glared at the white trousers strained round her thin shapely bottom as Vicky Barclay reached into the car for her shopping. She had gone out to buy a few extra items for the party as soon as they had arrived from London.

A plastic bag and a basket, overflowing with apples and three tins of mushroom pâté that she had bought as an afterthought, were balanced upright together on the grass so that she could talk to Ben.

She walked over to him. 'Hi there, Mr Pearce.'

Ben mumbled at her. He noticed that she wasn't wearing anything under her thin man's shirt because he could see the dark shadows her nipples made. Disgraceful hussy!

'And how's our Mr Pearce today?'

'Overworked,' he snapped.

His reply answered the question by pure chance.

'We're having a few people in for drinks this evening. I hope we don't disturb you.' Her smile was wide and forced.

'Drink! Caw. I wouldn't mind one of them.'

'Yes. Thirsty weather. Like some orange juice?'

He tilted one ear in her direction.

'Fresh orange juice,' she bellowed. 'Would you like some?'

'Wouldn't mind a cuppa tea. I'm fair sweating.'

'Right. Tea it shall be. Sugar?'

'Four lumps, missus. And strong.' Then, because a small feeling of unease nagged him, he added, 'Ta then.'

Vicky was going to repeat the bit about the party but changed her mind. The chances were that he wouldn't hear them anyway.

'Watch out, missus,' Ben said. 'Them ducks is after your things.'

The basket lay on its side, apples still rolling. Vicky ran forward to retrieve them while Blondie and three motionless drakes watched with their small eyes. She took the shopping through the wrought-iron gate that Jeff had attached to the wall where Ben's cottage joined theirs. Ben shuffled out to shoo Blondie away from the small round tin lying on the grass. He would give it to her when she came with the tea and she might be glad of a few leaves of spinach for her party. Then he remembered that she was after his cottage, bribing him with tea and her hubby's electric cutters. It didn't fool him! She could keep her blasted tea. He shoved the tin into his pocket. It would do for a bit of a change for his supper, whatever it was.

He left the gate open and, stamping over the hedge-cuttings that littered the path, went round his side of the cottage to his kitchen. On the grease-coated draining-board his electricity bill remained unopened. Pol had always paid the bills. Twice since she had died the man had come about the electricity, threatening to cut it off, and twice Ben had counted out the pound coins, sliding them into his cupped palm from the edge of the table. He kept them in a special jam-jar in the pantry. The shelves were stacked with cob-webby jars as he never threw anything out. He would never do away with useful things like that.

Ben muttered to himself that Mr Petherbridge down the road could see to it, for Adrian Petherbridge had taken it upon himself to pay Ben's electricity bill when he did his own. Out of habit Ben tore the paper into bits and added them to the rubbish-filled hearth in his living room.

He collected last Sunday's *News of the World* that Dolly

Wolfe had passed on to him that morning and took it to his outside privy. The sloping roof jutted from his kitchen and one wall formed part of the Barclays' boundary. This was extended by a wattle fence where an enthusiastic Clematis grew. Over the roof the cowl of an outlet pipe was only a few feet above one of the Barclays' windows. He was hardly aware of the stench that always increased in the hot weather. Charlie Wilson from the Council came regularly on Monday mornings to remove the container inside his privy and replace it with another.

Clutching the newspaper so that he could have a good read before using it, he disappeared inside, leaving the door half-open for light.

Although Jeff Barclay was on the patio at the other side of the wattle fence he did not hear Ben because he was stretched out on a padded recliner asleep. They usually left London on Friday evening for a quick dash to the cottage but yesterday the Porsche had been booked in for a service and they had been unable to get away until early that morning. Despite the clear run he was tired.

He had brought in cooler boxes full of meats and salads and struggled up the drive carrying frail plastic bags heavy with gin and whisky and large bottles of mixers.

'Where's that box marked "gooey and fragile"?' said Vicky. 'Don't tell me I've left it behind.'

'I've just dropped it on the path.'

'*Jeff!*'

'Joke, darling, joke. I was very careful.'

'You'd better be.'

'You've got far too much food here.'

Vicky had taken the car out to buy some more, wailing before she left that there was a giant spider in the sink. It *was* a large spider. Jeff had turned on the tap and watched the creature try to climb the slippery sides in panic. When the rising water lapped at its scrabbling legs the spider had curled itself into a ball and floated away. After it had jerked down the plughole Jeff turned off the tap and looked at his watch. It was still only half past ten but he'd been up since six and needed a reviver.

The chink of ice against the side of the tumbler relaxed him. He carried the garden recliner into the shade of the Clematis, took off his shirt and lit a cigarette. Twittering swallows dived about over his head, a gentle soothing noise. Bees buzzed among the Jackmanii that Vicky had planted beside the wattle fence. She had been furious to discover that the largest blooms, growing high to reach the sun, had toppled on to Ben Pearce's side where they hung in a glorious mauve tangle. Poor old Vicky. Jeff couldn't care less but he made sympathetic noises.

This is what it's all about, he thought, taking a cool sip of gin. He had owned the place for two years now, gutting and rebuilding the interior to his own design. Vicky had visited auctions and junk shops buying furniture which she stripped and polished to a fashionable straw colour. She ferreted out bric-à-brac which in his eyes had no merit until it was displayed on some shelf in the cottage.

That gin had been quite strong. He had it in mind to construct a small swimming pool, enclosed by a high brick wall, to trap the sun and keep off the north wind. If some of the hedge at the side was removed Charlotte could nip through from her place and swim whenever she fancied, even when they were in London. It was lucky that their garden extended to hers behind Ben's scruffy plot. Jeff smiled as he imagined the water creeping up her soft, voluptuous body. His eyes flickered and he slept.

The next thing he heard was Vicky flinging open the window above him to toss out a handful of small flies that had danced themselves to death on the glass panes.

'Lucky for some,' she called.

'Leave it, can't you. Get yourself a drink and come out.'

'At this hour? Someone's got to get going for the party.'

'Expecting high jinks in the bedroom, are you?'

'Funneee! Don't forget to make some fresh ice.' She flapped the duster like a yellow flag and vanished inside.

Hassle, hassle, what was wrong with the ice already in the fridge? The cottage was supposed to be a place for relaxation. This party was all her idea and quite unnecessary as they did more than enough entertaining in town. Her vivacity, which had attracted him in the first place, he often found exhausting now. A baby would absorb some of her surplus energy. Vicky wanted a baby. The doctor at the infertility clinic she had visited last year told her that he could not find anything wrong. She was to return in a year if she did not become pregnant.

Jeff knew that he was not to blame because he had been married twice before, once when he was only twenty. He had been infatuated until he discovered his first wife could keep up a silent mood for a week in between the rows — during which time she was over-communicative. After a year she had taken the child and gone off to live with some other guy. His solicitor had dealt with all the maintenance or whatever, and never bothered him.

His second wife had just been bloody unreasonable. Jane had left him when she found out about Kiki Hunt and had made a great drama out of it. The absurd thing was that it had never been as serious with Kiki as with some of those girls she didn't know about. He would like to have watched the twins grow up although he did see the boys from time to time, when they were allowed to come under his evil influence. Vicky was very good with them.

She reappeared at the window to remind him not to forget to ring Lord Flora Dora. Irritated, Jeff refused to turn his head. He had invited Dick out to lunch on Monday and had to confirm it. Despite the fact that Vicky despised Dick Butterfield's questionable methods of running his empire, her usual commendable efficiency had got the better of her. In fact she had reminded him twice already. That man had a talent Jeff admired and Vicky was not going to influence his business relationships.

Suddenly Jeff gulped down his drink. He left the garden, disturbing the mallards as he crossed the bridge on his way to say hello to Charlotte.

At the quacking Vicky turned to the window that looked across Ben's garden to the road. When Jeff was out of sight she hung his white towelling bathrobe on the bedroom door and sat on the bed in a despondent mood. Damn Charlotte Franklin!

Outside Ben started to sweep his path with a slow monotonous swish and a phlegmy cough. Damn Ben Pearce! The sooner their cottage included that old fool's next door the better. Already Jeff had offered to buy the place, only to be subjected to a torrent of abuse. He hadn't been put out. 'Calm yourself down,' he'd said, 'don't get in such a state. That cough of his will finish him off sooner or later.'

She had argued that it was possible Ben could hang on for another ten years. Some of these country types were practically indestructible. Just be patient, was all Jeff kept saying.

To cheer herself up she began to plan what she would do with the end cottage. She'd chuck out the privet and turf the front for a start. The cauliflowers could be buried away under Italian tubs overflowing with fuchsias and Begonias and that trailing blue stuff whose name she could never remember. How much longer were they going to be forced to tolerate the smell of those bloody rotting cauliflowers and that stinking privy, not to mention the sight of filthy washing that drooped on the line for days on end? Worst of all was the ritual that she and Jeff were forced to endure every night. They were wakened by the slide of a sash window in Ben's bedroom followed by a spattering on the gravel behind their gate. It was nothing short of obscene.

Angrily she got up and took some fresh soap to the bathroom.

Kenneth shouted to Cat to tell her that the taxi had arrived. She was adamant that he should not drive her to the station at Lynn because she said the opportunity to get acquainted with a clutch of locals at the party was too good to miss.

'Who knows, you might meet some fantastic creature,' she said.

'Fat chance! Have a good trip and take one or two nice snaps for me.'

'Right. And you look after Toshy and don't let the dreaded Steinway bully you.'

The driver slammed her door. She lowered the window. 'Wish you were coming.'

'So do I,' said Kenneth. 'I would if I weren't so busy.'

'Don't forget to turn off the immersion heater.'

'No, darling.'

'Close the windows and empty the pedal-bin.'

'*Yes*, darling.'

'And dust the clock.'

She was laughing as she wound up the window. She bunched her lips into a noisy kiss as the car drove away.

5

The Petherbridges were in Vicky's kitchen getting under her feet. Jeff had given them each a drink and Vicky had put her conversation on to automatic while her mind concentrated on the last tasks still to be attended to.

Carol and Adrian Petherbridge always arrived early when they were invited out, disrupting the hostess's last few precious minutes, and then left early, departing noisily, filling the other guests with unease in case they were outstaying their welcome.

When Vicky answered the door, Carol saw that she had not changed yet as she was wearing a lemon jumpsuit, pulled in tight about the waist with a narrow gold belt. Her sandals were held on by a single gold strap and a variety of gold chains chinked around her neck and wrists. Later, when she remained as she was, Carol felt frumpish in her silk two-piece, although she knew her figure was still good and her uncomfortable high-heeled shoes had been expensive. Adrian disliked her in high heels as it made her taller than he was.

'Excuse me if I carry on.' Vicky grabbed a knife to chop some parsley. 'Do sit down.'

'I prefer to stand,' said Carol.

'Jeff, pull out a chair for Carol.'

'She prefers to stand,' said Adrian. 'In case she misses anything.'

He brushed one hand over his pale receding hair while he looked at Jeff for approval but got none.

Carol tilted her head away from him. Her eyes flickered over the pine units and the dark blue Aga in its tiled alcove.

Blue tiles on the worktops reflected the sweet-jars, with ground-glass stoppers, full of Barbados sugar and pasta shells and kidney beans. There were blue casseroles, blue mugs on hooks and a blue-handled washing-up brush. Carol had always thought blue a cold colour.

A swollen blue and white teapot stood on the floor minus its lid. She picked it up, thinking it must be there by mistake.

'I've got a load of dried grasses somewhere to stuff in that.' Vicky gazed around her. 'The last lot scattered seeds everywhere.'

'It's Delft,' said Carol.

'Right. Part of a breakfast-set a friend gave us. A wedding present.'

'Unfortunately the guy couldn't make the reception because he was enjoying a free compulsory holiday,' said Jeff.

'Prison!' Adrian felt pleased that he had caught on so quickly.

Carol gave a small laugh, convinced that it was a joke.

'We sent him a larger than usual piece of cake,' said Jeff.

'Jeff, could you shift your bum away from the sink for one minute.' Vicky waved a parsley-encrusted finger.

'Sorry, darling.' He banged ice-cubes out of a metal container while he whispered something improper in her ear.

Carol sniffed and turned her attention to the dresser. Beside the remaining piece of the Delft breakfast-set, she noticed a tiny Victorian doll sitting with legs outstretched. It had a black-painted cap of hair and eyebrows thin as cotton, on a face that was pitted and grey. Carol picked it up. The lower parts of its arms and legs were china, attached to upper limbs and a thinly stuffed body of fabric. Small china heels were extensions of its feet. Any clothes it once wore had rotted away many years before. Germ-laden, thought Carol. And not even attractive.

She reddened when Jeff, who did not appear to be watching her, called out, 'Sexy, isn't she?'

'Most unusual.' Carol replaced the doll before brushing her fingertips delicately together. She had always been aware that she was over-sensitive to dirt. Curiosities like that made her skin creep and a room where food was prepared was certainly no place to keep them.

As the doorbell rang for the second lot of visitors, Carol pulled a tissue from her handbag and, without thinking, rubbed away a smudge that clouded the glowing knob on a drawer.

Peter Lawrence was being talked to by the local mushroom farmer. In repose Leonard Graham's face was not unlike a self-portrait that Peter's son, Nick, had drawn long ago, the mouth curled like a new moon on its back, under a balloon nose and two hooded eyes. Leonard's unattractive features became transformed into a pleasant, sympathetic face, when animated – as they were now as he described how his electric razor had ceased in mid-whirr, leaving his head with a tendency to tilt, pulled down by the weight of the unshaven stubble.

This was the third time he had related the story that evening, improving the words to sharpen the image they conjured up at each telling. Now his intention was not only to amuse. Peter grinned politely as he waited for the inevitable question. Leonard wanted him to repair the razor.

Leonard took it for granted that friends, or even acquaintances, would perform little favours for him, just as he would for them if he were asked.

'You must let me look at the thing,' said Peter.

'Oh, that would be kind,' said Leonard. 'It's probably something quite simple and even if it isn't I know you'll be able to fix it.'

'I'll try.'

Peter found the repairing of electrical faults a challenge, giving him a feeling of real achievement when the problem was solved. In his house, appliances rarely misbehaved and those that dared to falter were quickly brought under control with a poke from a screwdriver or a wallop from the flat of his hand.

'I'll drop it round some time, shall I?' said Leonard.

'Right,' said Peter.

Kate came across the grass to where Vicky and Adrian Petherbridge were looking at some rose-bushes. She was wearing a skirt and top of Emma's that Rosemary had found and her hair was fastened back with a tortoiseshell and diamanté hairclip. In one hand she carried a bowl of potato sticks, glad to have something useful to do.

Adrian drew in his breath sharply. 'This has black spot,' he said, lifting a speckled yellow leaf.

'Chicago Peace,' said Vicky. 'Aren't the blooms fantastic!'

'They won't be. Spray,' said Adrian, pompously. 'Get Propiconazola or better still dig the lot out and burn them.'

'Oh, I couldn't do that. I'll buy whatever you said some time.'

Adrian took a handful of potato sticks. 'The spores lie about, you know, on the ground, ready to reinfect. Disastrous!'

'Do they?' Vicky remembered that she had not told Mrs Wolfe where she could find the clean tea towels.

'These are nice.' Adrian crunched potato sticks in his open mouth. 'We have rabbits. Do you?'

'Yes,' said Vicky. 'There was a young one feeding on the grass last time we were here. Gorgeous!'

'Kill it,' boomed Adrian. 'Vermin, my dear girl. You must kill it.'

'Oh, surely one little— '

'You must put sentiment aside. They eat all my vegetables and lie about on my flowers.'

'We've only got a few tubs and the roses.'

Adrian seemed unaware that she had spoken. 'I'll come in while you're in town and see what I can do for you.'

'Please don't bother,' said Vicky. 'I know how busy you are.'

'A net and a bit of chicken wire. That'll do it. I've caught quite a few in nets. Then . . . ' He twisted his clenched hands in opposite directions and clicked his tongue.

'How's your glass?' said Vicky. 'Let Kate get you a refill.'

'Gin and tonic and another slice of lemon but no ice this time.'

As Kate returned to the house Vicky propelled him towards a retired couple who where gazing silently at the other guests like an audience watching a play. When she turned her back she heard Adrian inquire if they were troubled by rabbits.

His shouting voice was loud enough to carry over the fence to Ben Pearce, who was crouching by the Clematis peering through a hole in the wattle.

Jeff took Dilly Harris to a low armchair where she flopped down, knowing that she would not be able to rise again without help because of her arthritic knees. She was quite capable of standing like everyone else, at least to begin with, and she had wanted to join a group of people where the man from the mushroom farm was telling a tale. But Jeff was adamant. Now her breadth of vision was further restricted because her eyes were on a level with the back of the mushroom farmer's knees.

Jeff came across, bringing a glass of amontillado. He lit a cigarette for her and left again. She would have preferred him to have brought someone interesting to talk to or at least a sweet sherry. Why did he assume she drank medium? She looked about the parts of the room she could see. Although her eyes were partly hidden behind wrinkled lids, they were as alert and watching as a bird's.

In the alcove beside the fireplace, three shelves were crammed with paperback books. The spines looked shiny and uncracked, which probably meant they were unread, Dilly decided. This was true. Vicky had wanted the shelves to have a furnished look as soon as they were fixed to the wall so she had collected a large number of paperbacks from a shop that sold remainders, mostly horror and soft porn. By the yard, Jeff had commented, adding that he hoped no one would see the lurid covers.

Dilly's books had dog-eared corners and covers that refused to lie flat. Now, as she leaned forward to read the authors' names, she realised that she had not heard of any of them, which surprised her. The contents would have surprised her even more, but not shocked her. Only if the writing was bad enough to be tiresome would she close a book unfinished. Otherwise she gobbled up any reading matter that came her way. Quite often she finished a complete novel in a night when she was unable to sleep. At the moment she was part of the way through *Bleak House* and a collection of Irish short stories and was just about to begin on a John Mortimer novel from the library.

'Hello.'

Dilly looked up to see a man towering above her.

'I'm Kenneth Weaver. Mind if I join you?'

'No, there's nice.' Dilly introduced herself. Her voice had a trace of Welsh in the vowels.

He sat on the arm of her chair. She guessed he was about forty. Thick, springy curls covered his head and as he smiled his teeth looked very white against his short, dark beard.

Dilly said, 'You're a handsome young man.'

'Never go by appearances,' he said. 'I'm a criminal hiding from the law.'

'Really!'

'Certainly! Do you know everyone here?'

'Yes.' Dilly was not able to see many people, but she expected this to be so if they all came from the village. 'But I don't know you. Are you married?'

'I am. I saw my wife off in a taxi this afternoon.'

'A taxi! To where?'

'King's Lynn. She flying to Greece.'

'There's no airport at Lynn. I hope she is aware of that. Do you know, I've never flown!' Dilly brushed a trail of cigarette ash from her chest. 'I will yet.'

Kenneth told her about their move to the lodge. Twenty

minutes later they had discovered that they had a mutual interest in Scrabble, the novels of Jane Austen and the wool-churches of North Norfolk.

Not far away Carol was describing the symptoms and terminal illness of someone Rosemary didn't know. She was finding it difficult to stop her eyes sliding away from Carol's gaze to a watercolour behind her head. When Carol had killed off her patient she turned to discover what was catching Rosemary's attention.

'I always thought I could be quite a good painter if I took the trouble to concentrate on it,' she said.

'You should,' Rosemary replied with no enthusiasm as she'd heard this excuse before.

'I was always good at school. Watercolour isn't as messy as oils.'

'Just as difficult though.' Rosemary was trying to read the artist's name. 'Come out with me some time.'

'Yes, I think I just might.'

'You can share my paints. How about one day next week?'

'Next week! Oh, life's a bit hectic at the moment.'

'Some other time then,' said Rosemary, with an inward sigh of relief. 'I've been offered an exhibition at the gallery in Rington. That's if I can get enough work together in time.'

'Very nice.' Carol's tone of voice turned Rosemary's news into a boast.

Kate came by, her attention focused on a slice of lemon bobbing about on top of the over-full glass of gin and tonic she was carrying. She had been talking to Jeff for so long at the drinks-table that it was a wonder Adrian had not come in search of his drink.

'I hope that's not yours, Kate,' said Rosemary.

'It is not. It's for that eejit who strangles rabbits.'

'Oh dear! Having a good time?'

'Yes, I am,' Kate's green eyes sparkled. 'A great time!'

'Quaint little thing,' said Carol, before she was out of earshot. 'All that hair. And that appallingly long skirt. Still,

40

like you, it must be nice not to have to worry about fashion.'
Carol pouted her mouth to take a sip of orange juice.

'I've more important things to do,' said Rosemary, calmly.

'I suppose that girl was referring to my husband, he's neurotic about those rabbits. Obsessed to the point of lunacy.'

'Surely not.' Rosemary thought Carol relished the chance to run him down.

'Our place is fortified with chicken wire. It takes an age to get in and out of our drive, unrolling the stuff to get the car through. And still the wretched creatures get in.'

Only half-listening as Carol prattled on, Rosemary watched Kate come in from the garden and go upstairs.

Charlotte paused between two hanging baskets overflowing with fuchsia and trailing ivy on either side of the Barclays' front door. It was open a crack and by the noise she guessed that she was last again. The booms from the low register of the muzak accompanied a chorus of twittering voices.

Before she walked in Charlotte took one end of the black, cobwebby shawl lying across her shoulders and tossed it round the neck of the black dress that fluttered around her like a thin, voluminous nightdress. Jeff slid past his guests in an effort to reach her, but Vicky was already ushering her on to the patio to talk to Kate.

'Hi, lovey, how did the collecting go?' asked Charlotte.

Kate smiled, showing her small even teeth. 'Great, but there's more to do.'

'Good luck. Not a job I'd enjoy.'

A tall man with a wide stomach joined them. 'And where's that fine-looking son of yours? Is he here?'

'No, Major. Too busy chasing birds.'

He gave a great roar of laughter. 'Not a bad occupation.'

That I deserved, thought Charlotte, asking him for a cigarette. He pulled out his lighter and flicked up the flame in an elaborate gesture.

'I'm sure they're no prettier than his mother.'

41

Charlotte turned to Kate. 'You must meet Colin, lovey. He hasn't got any friends of his own age. He's a bit of a loner. You'll do him good.' She leaned forward to whisper, 'You should have brought a pocket full of charity envelopes. You would have done well here.'

When Kate smiled, her green eyes became slits like those of a contented cat.

As Ben walked beside the hedge that divided his land from Charlotte's, a movement under the hawthorn twigs made him stop abruptly. He bent his head to listen. A loud rustle was audible even to his deaf ears. He dropped the bucket he was carrying to upend his broom and, repeatedly shouting, 'Gid out of it!' thrashed about battering down the grass and cracking the nettle stems. A terrified rabbit fled into Charlotte's garden. Ben stopped and waited until he had satisfied himself that no other creature remained hidden in the undergrowth. Puffing with exertion and anger he picked up the bucket and went to collect hedge-clippings. He saw the cars parked haphazardly all over the grass in front of his cottage. Resisting the impulse to throw stones at them in case anyone was watching, he filled his bucket instead and shuffled laboriously back, spilling green leaves and earth along the path until he reached the Clematis.

The wattle fence had a crack in the centre. Six months ago he had widened it, jabbing away with the blade of a knife when the Barclays were in London. Now that the Clematis had grown up he made sure of an unrestricted peephole by keeping it clear of foliage and purple flowers on their side as well as his.

He paid frequent visits to their garden when the house was empty, misting up the window-panes as he leaned on the sill, his face hovering over the glass. The blinds and curtains were always drawn and he saw nothing except a ewer decorated with pink flowers standing in its matching bowl on the wide ledge inside. A queer place for them, he considered, when the bedroom was upstairs. Once, one of the chair-beds had been left out by mistake and he had lowered himself creakily on to the soft cushions. Mrs Wolfe had caught him at it and said she would tell Mrs Barclay but she never did.

The chink that he had made in the wattle fence was wide enough for both eyes. Through it he saw Adrian Petherbridge talking non-stop. In between rapid sips of drink his lips moved like a pair of damp worms while the couple from the main road couldn't get a word in edgeways. Ben tossed a handful of privet over the fence before he tipped the rest behind a row of spinach.

Finally, he went to the fence for one more look. If he could not hear what they were saying there was no reason why they should not hear him. The television stood in the corner of the living room. He turned it on so that the sound was up to its full volume, booming even louder than he needed it. A comedian from the north was telling coarse jokes which were followed by a roar of audience laughter. He slid the sash window up and propped the kitchen door wide open with a chair and then sat down, resting his back on the grubby grey-and-black-striped ticking of the pillow he used as a cushion.

It gave him enormous pleasure to know that everyone at the party could hear it too.

Through the dividing wall Vicky listened to the blast of the television. She discovered Jeff by the fireplace, where he had succeeded in getting Charlotte to himself at last.

'For God's sake! Do something,' whispered Vicky in a fury. She hammered on the wall.

'Calm down,' said Jeff. 'Calm down, sweetheart.'

'Just go next door and shut him up, Jeff.'

Carol came over, calling, 'Leave him to me. He owes me a favour, several in fact.'

'Let me go.' Charlotte blew a puff of grey smoke into the air before she stubbed her cigarette out. 'Have you got a beer I can take him?'

Twenty minutes later the television was silent and Charlotte had returned.

'Well done,' said Jeff.

Charlotte smiled. 'Poor old boy. He said "ta" for the beer.'

'Never worry about the inevitable,' Dilly was saying to Kenneth. 'What are these green slices in my salad?'

'Kiwi fruit.'

'There's posh.' Dilly waved her spoon upwards. 'Have you seen our sunsets? Something to do with the atmosphere. At times the sky is the colour of blood and the sun is twice its normal size. Of course it only appears like that, mind.'

Kenneth said he was looking forward to seeing one.

'They're best in October. What do you think to our ducks?'

'A bit stubborn about moving off the road for cars.'

'Quite fearless. Even tractors don't intimidate them.'

'Don't they get run over?'

'Occasionally. Now I do hope you don't read the dictionary when you're checking the spelling of a seven-letter word.'

'Never,' said Kenneth, amused that he could follow the drift of her grasshopper conversation.

'Good. So we'll visit Snettisham Church, is it? Llandaff Cathedral is my favourite, mind, but I haven't been there for forty years.'

Jeff had come to lean apologetically over Dilly so that he could draw the curtains, paying careful attention to a pair of ancient kitchen scales and its pyramid of weights on the window-ledge.

He said, 'It's getting quite dark outside.'

The guests were moving indoors, crowding the room even more. Jeff heard Adrian Petherbridge announce to everyone that he and Carol must think about going.

'Is that the gentleman with the wire fortifications across his drive?' asked Kenneth.

'That's him,' said Jeff. 'Lives right opposite you, doesn't he?'

'Yes. How does he manage when he has things to be delivered.'

'I think the stuff gets chucked over regardless.'

44

Their laughter made Dilly look up. Jeff took her dish. 'More fruit salad?'

'No, thank you.' Dilly spat on her finger to rub at a pink drip on her bodice. 'I enjoyed that, except for the raspberry pips. I don't expect you're bothered by a plate, are you, dear?'

She was interrupted by Adrian shouting across the head of the mushroom farmer for Carol.

Ben sat in his chair facing the silent television which he hadn't touched since Mrs Franklin had turned it down when she came in for a chat. After she had closed the window and the door she said she had brought him a can of beer from the party next door, which she opened for him and poured into a chipped glass. She had picked up the tin he'd found on the grass and asked him if he liked mushroom pâté. He told her he didn't know, he was going to try a bit for his supper. She noticed his slippers on the table and slid his feet into them after she had unlaced his boots and pulled them off. Then, kneeling by his side, she took his hand and talked into his ear as she apologised for the noise next door and hoped it wasn't bothering him. He caught a whiff of her scent and felt the warmth of her fingers. Her beetroot-coloured nails didn't look at all bad, he considered, although he didn't usually approve of that sort of caper.

They had talked about Pol and she said she'd never had a cleaning lady as thorough and as willing as Pol and the garden had gone to pot since he'd stopped coming to clear the rough. Just before she left she promised to let him have some indigestion powders that had done the trick when she had overeaten recently. Charlotte had occasional binges when she felt depressed about her diet.

Nice woman, one of the best, that Mrs Franklin, he thought when she had gone. She talked to you like a mate. She was genuine, not a bit of side. He felt more cheerful than he had done for a long time. Her scent was still about the room.

Despite his antagonism towards Colin, Ben had always

45

had a different attitude towards the boy's mother. She had been generous when Pol had worked for her. Pol had always returned home in a communicative frame of mind, her eyes shining behind the small frames of her spectacles, repeating what Mrs Franklin had said about this and that.

Once, Charlotte had given her a plastic frog suspended on a chain. It stared with large, jutting eyes of crystal. Ben was convinced that they were valuable stones. After washing up the dinner things on Sunday, when she had changed into her best frock, Pol wore the frog on her great shelf of a bosom, where it crouched as if it were waiting for an opportunity to leap on to the carpet in the front parlour. She kept the pendant wrapped in tissue in a dressing-table drawer for the rest of the week, and there it had remained until this afternoon when he had taken it out.

Ben rested his head back. It hadn't been a bad sort of a day. He'd had several visitors, all welcome.

He was feeling a bit peckish. He picked up the tin and read the label. Mushroom pâté, whatever that was. He pulled the ring to release the top and sniffed. Not bad, a bit of a treat that would be. He cut himself a doorstep of bread, fetched an apple that had been withering on the draining-board for the past fortnight and sat at the table. Methodically he began to peel the apple, cursing the bluntness of the knife. His head nodded down and he fell asleep.

He woke suddenly with a start. Outside someone's knuckles thumped at the kitchen door. It took a minute for Ben to heave his stiff body into a standing position. He was aware that he was being watched through the curtainless window.

There was another knock. Ben half-hoped that Mrs Franklin had come back. He unbolted the door and opened it, drenching the figure outside with a cold light.

Flapping his hand at a moth that had fluttered in, Ben said, 'Hello. What you doing here at this time of night? Want to come in then?'

His visitor said something about the ducks without entering the kitchen.

Then Ben fetched a torch and followed the hurrying figure, past the moving shadows cast by the cauliflower curds and the forest of spinach leaves. The garden gate clicked shut when they had gone through it. A tawny owl called a sharp 'bewick' from the oak in Charlotte's garden before all the ducks began to quack.

PART TWO

6

The morning after the party Dilly was sitting in bed leaning back on three pillows because Dr Macey insisted that she slept upright. After a restless night her snowy hair had lost its pins and stuck up all round like a soft brush. She closed the book she had been reading for the past two hours, using a recent letter from her son as a bookmark.

When she switched on the radio beside her bed it emitted a discordant blare played on instruments she didn't recognise. Her new friend Kenneth would have enlightening views on the subject, as he seemed to have on everything. She must ask him. She turned the volume down while she waited for the news.

Today was important because the 9.30 service on Radio Four was being relayed from a chapel in Cardiff that she had attended as a child, three times a day every Sunday including Sunday school. On that day the food never varied, she remembered, boiled eggs for breakfast, a roast left to cook itself in the black range for one o'clock sharp, red jelly with bread and butter for tea and cocoa before bed. Even now Dilly still liked bread and butter whenever she had red jelly. And she became nostalgic each time she heard the humming glory of a Welsh choir. Inappropriately she began a throaty rendering of 'The day Thou gavest Lord is ended,' finishing after one verse when she remembered that it was *Sunday Times* day.

Dilly always tried to complete the crossword so that it caught the Monday post, although she had never won a prize. She swung her legs over the side of the bed, wriggling her feet into slippers with bobbles that her granddaughter had knitted for her in Paris. Dilly's daughter had married a French doctor and her son was an accountant in York.

As she passed the telephone on the way to the kitchen she rang Kenneth to ask if he knew where he could get the Sunday papers. He was a long time answering and his curt 'Hello' softened as he replied that, yes thank you, he did.

After she had filled the kettle she pulled a cup and saucer from last night's dun-coloured water and rinsed them under the tap. Tea-leaves from the pot were emptied down the sink where they bunched together like a gleaming brown plug. She dressed while the kettle boiled, returning to find the water cold because she had not switched it on.

'Dilys Blodwen Thomas, there's dull you are this morning!'

She had used her maiden name when talking to herself as a child and marriage to Edward Harris had not altered the habit. He had been a professor of medieval history at Cambridge. They had met walking in the Brecon Beacons.

It wasn't worth getting her bicycle out for such a short distance but, although she had not ridden it for many years, it was an option she always considered. Crunching along the gravel beside Ben's cottage she saw no sign of life at the Barclays. They would be too exhausted after the party, she imagined. A mallard dozed on the bonnet of their opulent motorcar. As she walked, Dilly's following of noisy pushing ducks thinned and lost interest until only Blondie stood in the road watching.

The sky had a pale translucent look that promised another scorching day. Above Dilly's head the tips of swallows' wings miraculously avoided each other as the birds curved in arcs catching flies.

On the other side of the wheatfield a man was running along the sea-wall. Dilly was sure it was Jeff Barclay jogging alone, so she had overestimated his need for sleep.

The Sunday papers were delivered to Fred Peddington, who lived in a small cottage beyond Charlotte's house. He stacked them in piles on one side of his narrow hall, ready for the steady trickle of people who began to call just before nine.

On the way home, where the road curved, Dilly saw that the notice which Adrian Petherbridge had hammered into the verge last winter to warn drivers – SLOW DUCKS – was faded and partly hidden by lush undergrowth. She made a mental note to do something about it. When she reached the bridge the ducks massed about her again so that she was obliged to move each foot carefully. She looked up to see Jeff coming towards her. He was no longer running and he was no longer alone. He had his arm around someone who was not his wife.

Oh, dear, thought Dilly, this is not right. But she prided herself on moving with the times and not becoming an old fuddy-duddy who criticised the behaviour of the younger generation, into which she bracketed anyone under sixty. She was reading too much into it. Yes, it was probably all quite harmless. They were completely absorbed in one another and had not noticed her. Just before she stepped on to her drive she saw Jeff stop to kiss the cheek of his laughing companion.

The kitchen was thick with steam from the boiling kettle. Eventually Dilly took a cup of tea and the section of the *Sunday Times* that held the crossword out on to the verandah. There, among the geraniums and the rooting African violets, she struck through the number of each clue as she answered it, while ash from her first cigarette of the day powdered the floor and a wrinkle of skin formed on the top of her tea.

7

The windows of the lodge were wide open, allowing the joyous sounds of a Haydn piano trio to carry over the dusty, neglected shrubs that ringed the small garden. Dilly's new friend was preparing for his trip out with her by pressing a recently washed, favourite shirt, in an attempt to dry it quickly. The noise of the hissing steam punctuated the recurring theme of the Gypsy Rondo. He unplugged the iron and leaned his pale hands on the board. He listened to the record not for the technical skill of the performers but for the pure nostalgia, and he despised himself for his indulgence. It was the sound of the piano that brought it all back.

Each bar of the music reminded him of the recording session. He and Cat had been at the studio in Maida Vale with the two string players. They had sat, side by side, the pianist and the page-turner on the edge of a chair ready to rise on silent, shoeless feet. Old Bossy Boots. He would never get used to these periods they were forced to spend apart. Wretched girl! He lifted the iron-creased sleeve of the shirt. Things went to pot when she was away.

The final chords of the rondo crashed out, the needle lifted and the turntable ground slowly to a halt. Kenneth took a chair outside and arranged the shirt around its wooden back to air in the sun. Then he saw Kate leaning over the garden gate.

Kenneth and Cat had seen the advertisement for the lodge one Sunday afternoon when the carpet was half-hidden under the tossed pages of the *Observer* flattened by their golden retriever, who dozed on top like a massive paper-weight. The tenancy of their London flat had almost run out and they were looking for somewhere to live. A nearly empty bottle of retsina stood on the floor beside Kenneth.

'Now how about this,' said Cat, as she read the advertisement, warmed by the wine. 'North Norfolk, to let, unfurnished, a lodge-cottage in a secluded position near the sea. Large living room, two bedrooms, kitchen, bathroom, small garden.'

'Ah, the small garden clinches it,' said Kenneth, emptying his glass.' I shall grow sweet musk roses and keep hens at the bottom.'

'Fool,' said Cat. 'Sounds idyllic just the same. Unfortunately it doesn't mention central heating.'

'Bad for your Steinway. I could cope with my thermal underwear,' said Kenneth. 'Where's your glass? Come on, drink up.'

'This plonk's not at all bad.' Cat drank her wine and held out her glass. 'Imagine leaving all the exhaust fumes and the hassle and the aggro. No threatening notes pushed under the door complaining about our musical racket. Doesn't that tempt you?'

'It does. But seriously, it would be out of the question.'

'Don't be so negative.' Cat went out to the car for a road map, leaving Tosca to whine with disappointment at the closed door.

'Look,' said Kenneth when she had returned. 'It's miles from London. We both need a base here. It's mad to even consider it.'

'Hang about.' Cat found the relevant page. 'Think of the money we'll save on rent.'

'We'll spend it all on petrol! And the time we'll waste!'

'Nonsense. The roads aren't all that bad. By-passes are being constructed all the time. Two hours and a bit, I reckon.'

The wet nose of the retriever pushed at the book on Cat's lap and Tosca looked into her face with mournful eyes. 'Not yet, Toshy. We're discussing your future.'

'Why this sudden passion for Norfolk?' asked Kenneth.

'No cracks about it being flat, now. We did go there once,' said Cat. 'I must ask Dad where it was.'

'By the sea?'

'No, inland somewhere.'

'Let's be serious though,' said Kenneth. 'It would be crazy to think about moving so far away.'

'No harm in looking. A nice day out. Anyway we must check that my dreaded Steinway will go in.'

'But of course,' said Kenneth. 'Shall I uncork another bottle?'

During the visit they had decided that the piano would fit in and with that settled and the sun lighting up the marsh and turning the creeks and pools to dazzling mirrors, they rented the lodge for a year.

The furniture arrived, including the Steinway, which was charged for separately and had its own wrappings and trolley and one extra man to cope with the weight. Despite the earlier calculations the removal men spent three hours easing it through the doors and hall and into the living room before they could screw on the legs and haul it upright.

'Do us a favour and give us a miss, mate, when you want to move out,' the boss said, leaving a pattern of sweaty fingerprints on the piano's glossy surface.

'Sorry about that,' said Kenneth, while Cat huffed and rubbed at the marks. 'You all did a great job.'

As the men left they stepped cautiously over the recumbent Tosca as she tore a packing box into small, wet pieces in the hall.

Kate was leaning over the closed gate so that she could stroke Tosca's silky head.

'Fantastic music,' she said. 'Made me want to dance.'

She looked cool and Kenneth could see that her appearance had improved although he could not have described what she wore to the party.

'You look very nice,' he said. She was dressed in a white

56

creation with an embroidered bodice and ribbons threaded round the skirt.

'Do you like my frock then?' she said. 'I borrowed Emma Lawrence's bike this morning and cycled into the town to buy it. There's a market on Sundays.'

She had plaited her hair, starting from high on the back of her head, and it fell over one shoulder like a thick honey-coloured rope.

'Your gorgeous dog longs for a walk,' she said, in a small pleading voice, although Tosca's closed eyes and motionless head uplifted in ecstasy suggested nothing of the kind. 'Will I take her for you?'

'Thanks but we both have a date with a very special lady. Tosca will have to be satisfied with a view from the back of the car.'

He hoped Kate would not ask if she could join them because a refusal might sound unconvincing as there was no reason why she should not come. Dilly would not mind, he was sure. Instinct and experience warned him that he must not encourage Kate.

'I hear your wife is away for a while.' she said. 'You'll be missing her.'

'I am.' Kenneth went indoors. When he came back later to collect the shirt Kate had gone.

Tosca appeared when she heard the roar of the car engine, rucking up the bath-towel that protected the back seat as she bounded in.

When Dilly opened the door it was apparent that she was not ready as she was wearing a white nylon petticoat.

'Did you hear the service from Cardiff?' she asked. 'Unfortunately I forgot and missed the first half. Never mind.'

Five minutes later she called Kenneth into the bedroom to fasten the buttons at the back of her dress.

'Titchy things,' she said, as his fingers made a meal of them. 'You must remember to undo them or I'll have to go to bed just as I am. Now have I got the right handbag?'

'Is this the one?'

'That's it.' She rootled inside a grubby, plastic portmanteau. 'Pevsner's book on Norfolk architecture. Do you know it? – it's good. Reading glasses, angina tablets.'

She closed the zip with a series of tigging jerks and they went out to the car.

8

Colin Franklin sprawled like a young colt over his mother's settee, his legs weighed down by size-eleven trainers extending over one end. Mr Puss lay on the curve of his stomach, paws curled under on his chest, dozing with slit eyes. Colin disliked cats generally but on those occasions when Mr Puss was in a worshipping mood the animal was tolerated.

Any visitor who saw the photograph of Colin in its tarnished, silver frame on Charlotte's mantelpiece would have assumed that he was like most boys of his age, yet the steady gaze in the portrait was misleading as he avoided eye contact. The serious expression was typical, however, for he rarely smiled, which was a pity, Charlotte remarked in one of her wittier moments, as it would charm his precious birds off the salt-marsh.

His skin had the tan of a farm-worker. Thick wiry hair and infrequent visits to the barber exaggerated the size of his head and only when it was plastered down after a shower did it lie flat. He was skinny, six feet two inches tall, twenty years old, and he could not read or write. He had hated all three of the private schools his parents had chosen for him, his father because he was impressed by the boys' apparent good behaviour and his mother because she liked the pretty uniforms. His education had been erratic as Charlotte frequently kept him at home, if she suspected he was off-colour or if the weather was threatening or if she needed his company. She needed it often after George died.

'They grow up so quickly,' she would say to people who knew. George, who left the house early and returned late, did not.

Charlotte claimed that Colin's bad attendance at school was the reason for his backwardness. His teacher doubted it. Even Dilly Harris, who had coached him patiently, using methods that had been a success with other slow children, had given up. Colin liked Dilly and often visited her.

He could write his name but had a fund of excuses which enabled him to avoid contact with the printed word. Charlotte still said, 'You could do it if you tried, lovey.' Secretly Colin found this comforting although he pretended it did not bother him either way. He presented to the world an attitude of sullen indifference.

He understood figures enough to use the tape-recorder that Charlotte had bought him with interest from the building society. His tapes consisted of birdsong, some commercial but mostly those he had recorded himself. Illiteracy had sharpened his senses. His memory was excellent. He had devised a system of filing tapes that would have been unintelligible to the most competent librarian, enabling him to find any tape he wanted. Then he would slide the tape into the machine, set the speed to fast forward, and watch with steady brown eyes until the spinning figures reached the number he required.

'How you work that thing I'll never know,' Charlotte said. Her mind was closed to anything she thought she could not grasp.

Colin's other mechanical passion was a computer game called Leaps, where he aimed to get a frog safely from one riverbank to another by means of objects drifting in the water as they travelled swiftly across the screen. One false jump made the computer emit an ear-piercing shriek that could be heard throughout the house. In a frenzy of button-tapping Colin attempted to improve his score.

His natural habitat, like the birds he studied, was the salt-marsh. In a hide on the nearby reserve he would sit motionless in the corner on a long wooden bench, skinnily folded like a half-opened penknife, as he gazed through one of the long, narrow windows. Encounters with other bird-watchers were inevitable but when his binoculars were clamped to his eyes, he became almost oblivious of their presence.

His mother appeared at the living room door.

'Hello, lovey,' she said. 'I didn't hear you come in.'

Colin remained silent as he scratched the top off a midge bite.

'See any nice birds?'

He jerked Mr Puss awake as he roughly stroked the cat's head. 'The marsh harrier was flying around over the reeds.'

'Marvellous!' Charlotte, who didn't know a marsh harrier from a cuckoo, said nothing else in case it was inappropriate.

The cat jumped down with a gentle thud, getting itself entangled in the folds of her long skirt as it wove around her legs.

'No,' she said. 'If you're all that hungry go out and catch something.'

'*Mother.*'

'Sorry, lovey. Try not to be so sensitive.' She went into the kitchen for a tin of Kit-e-Kat, shouting through the doorway, 'That party of Vicky's was good fun. You really should come to these affairs. There's a nice Irish girl staying at the Lawrences. Very pretty. Kate something.'

'I've seen her around.'

'You might just get on, don't you think?' Charlotte jabbed the cat-meat out of the tin with a fork. 'And Rosemary Lawrence said could you spare the time to cut their grass.'

'I might.'

'I think she'd appreciate it if you could do it soon, lovey.'

'She'll be lucky!'

Colin intended to do it soon because he needed the money to buy more tapes.

When the cat's mouth was delicately jerking at the food, Charlotte returned with an open can of bitter from the fridge, saying, 'And try to finish the job, Colin, won't you?' as she handed it to him.

He was indignant. 'I always do! Moan, moan. The old

bat can just piss off.' He tipped the can and took a long swig.

'Oh, Colin, I'm glad your father can't hear you talk like that. And another thing, sorry to go on, but do try not to antagonise poor old Ben.'

'You're not serious, Mother! He chucked a hulking great stone at me the other day – into our garden. Anyway—'

'Anyway what?'

'Oh, nothing. Got anything to eat? I'm hungry.'

The sound of hammering echoed round the hall of the lodge. Kenneth had promised Cat that he would hang her collection of photographs while she was away. As they varied in size they had to be positioned carefully and he still couldn't get over the fact that she trusted him enough to arrange them in an acceptable combination.

He huffed on the glass of one that she had taken of him and rubbed the smudges clear on his shirtfront. It was black and white. Cat nearly always took black-and-white photographs. She also had a few portraits of her long-dead relations in sepia or moth-grey. Carefully he lifted her grandmother, with four greats in front – or was it five? – in a large ornate frame which had white plaster showing through the chips and cracks on the gilding. Pale streamers hung from the lady's frilled cap. These and her pupils and ringlets had been clumsily touched up by the Victorian photographer. A hundred book-lice lay dead under the glass like tiny black seeds. This picture was the pride of Cat's collection.

Below it he hung a small group of four solemn women whose dismembered heads appeared to be floating in a mist. He had forgotten who they were and couldn't be bothered to lift them off the wall to read the information underneath. The only picture he found of real interest was a postcard-sized group that had been taken outside a village hall after Sunday school, Cat said, when Edwardian teachers in glorious hats and boys in knickerbockers had posed in the street. One small boy had been identified by a pencil cross. Kenneth wondered who he was.

He examined the contents of a packing case, flicking through the upended frames he still had to deal with: Cat's grandmother, an uncle, her father who was still alive and her mother who was not, and ten others. They would have to wait until she got back. Except the one of Tosca. He had just taken out the photograph of the golden retriever when he noticed Kate, arms folded, leaning in the open doorway.

She was wearing the ethereal dress embroidered in white. 'I'm here to find out what all the racket's about,' she said.

'Come right in. Want to look at our gallery?'

Kate examined the photographs in a silence that proclaimed she would never decorate her walls with such a weird selection. She grasped the hair behind her neck and pulled it slowly through one hand before she tossed it free. She stared at him with wide green eyes.

'That one would be very old. The one in the big ugly frame. It's very faded.'

'Yes. That's Cat's grandmother with four greats in the front. I think it's four.'

'The cat?'

'No. Cat's my wife. She's away.'

She turned and put her face close to his portrait. 'That's a great one of you. Pity it's in black and white. Nowadays you mostly see colour. They're bound to be better.'

He smiled.

'So what's funny then?'

'Nothing. Black and white is just different. Not better or worse but different.'

'I see you know a lot about it.'

She watched him line up the photograph of Tosca next to his own and mark the wall with a pencil, then she sat down on a balloon-backed chair close to him. When she lifted her head her soft mouth reminded him of Botticelli's Venus and her hair was a similar dull gold. Through the material, between the white embroidery and pearls and beads, he could see that she wasn't wearing anything underneath the bodice of her dress. He found himself disturbed by her presence which was both virginal and provocative.

He mistrusted her demure expression as he suspected that it was a calculated pose.

'Here, hold this for me,' he said sharply.

She took the picture and watched him hammering. 'I think people who keep funny old things are eejits. Look at the bugs under that glass. They're bound to be unhealthy. Will you let me see the rest of the house?'

'Go on then, while I finish putting up Toshy. You'll have to be quick because I'm going out.'

Kate walked through into the sitting room, which was long and narrow, two rooms knocked into one. A grand piano dominated one end of the room, pushed under the front window where the light was constricted by an overhanging laurel and a fringe of ivy leaves from a creeper that was rampant outside.

Musical scores were piled untidily on the piano and a single book lay open, marked with written comments in green Biro. A fringed Spanish shawl lay in a heap on the piano-stool. Nearby stood an antique music-stand, carved and polished, flanked by two large green candles in brass holders at the top. Kate thought it would be fun to light them but could find no matches.

Instead she called out, 'It's a great brute of a piano you have here!'

'Yes, it rules our lives a bit,' Kenneth shouted back. 'It belongs to my wife.'

'And there was I hoping for a tune. These books scattered all over the top. She must be a terror. Will I tidy them for you?'

Kenneth's reply was lost in a burst of hammering. She turned away. When he came in she was on her hands and knees beside a shelf of records and music tapes.

'Done,' he said.

'I'd like a tape for my Walkman.'

'Have you got one of those infernal machines? Ruin your ears you know.'

'It's new,' said Kate, reading the title on a plastic box. 'I got it from the market.'

She asked what he had been playing when she came before. That was a record, he said, and rather precious. He lent her a tape of Hungarian dances. She took it to the other end of the room, passing a cardboard box full of unpacked books that had been pushed half into the grate of the ornately tiled fireplace. A clock in a heavy wooden case ticked from the mantelpiece. A patterned settee and two armchairs formed an intimate seating area around the fire. Kate squeezed between the arms to reach the rug they encircled, where Tosca was sprawled on her side apparently asleep until she opened her eyes. The dog scrabbled to her feet unbalancing Kate into a chair as she leapt over the back of the settee.

'*Tosca!*' bellowed Kenneth. 'Sorry she's so boisterous.'

Kate laughed, exposing small white teeth, and curled her legs round on to a cushion. Above a desk on the wall facing her she noticed a painting of pin-men hurrying in front of a factory with tall, smoking chimneys. She could draw more realistic figures than that, she thought, even though she was hopeless with a pencil.

'Black-and-white photos and paintings by children,' she said. 'Someone should have taken you in hand long ago.'

When Kenneth had gone out of the room she borrowed another tape from the shelf, holding it concealed in her palm close against her skirt so that he would not see it.

After he had shown her out Kenneth went upstairs to pack.

9

Charlie Wilson, with a bride of one month, was the young man who emptied Ben Pearce's waste-bucket. At eleven o'clock on Monday morning he jumped out of the lorry at the bridge to clap away the ducks while his driver, in low gear, inched his way through the hazards he was unable to see quacking around the wheels of his vehicle.

Charlie jammed open Ben's gate with a kick and loped along the path, swinging the clean container. Marriage had introduced a new urgency into his work. If he got off early he could finish putting the brass handles on to the Do-It-Yourself fitted wardrobe he had been putting together over the weekend. He'd promised Michelle that he would.

Charlie poked his head inside Ben's kitchen to glance around.

'Mornin' Ben,' he shouted. He guessed that Ben was glad of a chance of human contact if only for a minute.

A pint of milk stood on the doorstep. Charlie was always on the alert for the possibility of sickness or an accident when he went to the houses of the elderly. Only last year he had looked through one window to see the thin legs and red carpet-slippers of an old dear who had collapsed on her kitchen floor. It was a stroke, the doctor had said after complimenting Charlie on his vigilance. She was coming on well now.

He put down his bucket and went inside. What a tip! Above his head a bare electric light-bulb glimmered in the sunlight. It was unlike Ben, who they said was as tight as a tick, to leave it switched on. Charlie went through to the living room, walking on a wrinkled and rucked carpet that was more patterned with stains than flowers. Screwed-up papers overflowed on to it from the grate and hearth. The television screen fluttered palely with no sound.

On the table stood half a glass of beer, the surface made lumpy by three dead wasps and a partly opened tin of something. A thick slice of bread and an apple, turned ginger-brown where Ben had peeled away the skin, filled a small plate. Mouse-droppings surrounded it.

Charlie picked up the tin to read the label. He could hardly credit the contents: mushroom pâté. Old Ben was getting extravagant tastes in his old age.

Charlie became worried. He called Ben's name. He went to the room at the front of the cottage where the few articles of furniture had been pushed to one half of the carpet. The remainder was rolled back, exposing splintered floorboards and the damp earth underneath.

Poor old boy, thought Charlie. He must give him a hand with that floor, he knew a chap who would let him have a couple of planks cheap. It wouldn't take a morning to cut them to size and screw them down. It could all be done for free. After all the money he and Michelle had spent on that fitted wardrobe he'd be ashamed to take a penny.

Outside in the road the driver hooted. Charlie returned to the stairs that rose, narrow and steep, between two walls in the centre of the house.

'Ben, you up there, mate?' Suddenly he became alarmed. The thought of finding a corpse made his skin creep. He'd never seen anyone dead. He climbed the steep treads to a small landing that was flanked by two doors. The one leading to the room with a distant view of the sea was open. On the double bed lay a grubby candlewick spread crushed by three damp cardboard boxes grossly overfilled and misshapen. Through the grey window-panes Charlie could see the wheatfield glowing warm in the sun.

He went into the second room. This was where Ben must sleep. Army blankets had been hauled across the narrow bed. Charlie thought of the cream and pink duvet Michelle's mother had given them as a wedding present, the cream carpet he had bought on the never-never and the pale drapes, as Michelle called them. He looked through Ben's uncurtained window on to the drive that belonged to those weekenders from London. On the ledge outside bright green lichen thrived.

Charlie heard footsteps downstairs.

'Ben. That you?' he called.

'What you doin' up there?' the driver bellowed.

Charlie came sideways down the awkward stairs.

'Gettin' nosy in your old age, eh?' said the driver.

'No, I was lookin' for old Ben Pearce.'

'Gone down the shop, I expect. Come on, boy.'

'This place is falling apart. See the holes in this floor here.'

The driver followed Charlie.

'Caw,' he said, leaning forward, hands on knees. 'You could break a leg down that.'

'He left a couple of lights on.'

'You never left a light on then?'

'And telly. And food all over the table.'

'You got the wrong job, boy. Better join the fuzz. You emptied that bucket yet?'

'Not yet.'

'Get your skates on then. That little wife of yours'll be goin' off the boil.' He cackled.

'Shut it!'

As they went into the garden Charlie agreed that Ben had probably gone to Betty Tiller's shop. When he climbed into the lorry he noticed a boy, pelting the ducks with bread.

Ten-year-old William Graham was out early, feeding the mallards stale crusts. He hadn't had anyone to play with since his best friend had left for a holiday in Spain last Friday.

William was unable to move because of the pressing crowd of ducks that reached up to wave their bills at him, emitting soft demanding quacks and stamping painfully on his bare feet in their greed. Only when a piece of bread slipped between the feathers to the ground did the nearest heads disappear, hidden by the jostling bodies, until one of them grabbed it.

Once his supply of bread had run out they lost interest and waddled away. William stood for a minute looking for something to amuse him. Across the road, hanging from the trunk of a tree, he saw a small, cracked branch so he went over to snap it off. He tossed it from the bridge into the fast moving water where it floated out of sight underneath. Then, resting his cheek on the warm stone parapet, he watched for it to emerge on the other side. Pooh-sticks was pretty boring if there was no one to compete with, he thought, anyway it was a little kids' game. A duck with pale feathers, different from the others, stood in the road watching him.

'Quack,' said William. 'Quack, quack, quack.'

The branch did not appear so he assumed that it was caught up somewhere below. He did not really care about losing it but he was curious to know why it had not floated out on the other side of the bridge.

He went down the dusty bank and waded along the edge of the narrow river. At every step the water made a churning sound against his thighs. There were shadows under the bridge speckled with reflected light. One foot went down on a sharp-edged stone and he winced. He could see his branch stuck in the angle of a small wall of bricks at the far end. It seemed to be caught by something that looked like a half-submerged football, made green with a covering of weeds and surrounded by an accumulation of debris.

When he was close enough he reached out to free the branch. As he could not dislodge it he started to tug at the rubbish with both hands, throwing pieces of waterlogged wood and ribbons of vegetation aside. The ball, and what appeared to be a larger object attached to it, began to swing round. Slowly the ball twisted in the dancing light. Two staring weed-clogged eyes rose up and an open mouth emptied itself of water.

For a moment the boy remained still, paralysed with horror. Then he turned in a frantic attempt to get away but was unable to push his legs fast in the restraining current. It was like running through syrup. He went forward sobbing and tumbling. At last he came out from the shadow of the bridge into the warm air. He climbed the bank and fell sprawling on the grass, scattering the uneasy ducks. He lifted his head and was sick.

PART THREE

10

Warmed by the early-morning sun, Rosemary sat on the grassy sea-wall overlooking the old harbour, painting. She was waiting for a blue wash, which she had brushed completely over the paper, to dry before she continued.

The tide was high, concealing the soft mud in the narrow creek, and the road beyond it shone with pools. On the other side a second creek was less silted up, providing narrow access to the open sea for six small boats moored there. They floated in the water, straightened by the high tide, on their upside-down reflections. If Rosemary turned her head a little she could see, across the reed-bed, part of Marsh House through the gap in the trees that Peter had cleared. The continuous harsh churr of sedge-warblers came from deep in the reeds.

Using the tip of her finger Rosemary tested the paper for wetness. It was still damp. She was finding it difficult to concentrate. Ben's death had saddened everyone, except those who went about saying it was a happy release. But even they agreed it was a terrible business. Apparently the old man had slipped, possibly while feeding the ducks, pitched forward into the water and drowned. The current had carried him under the bridge. It was being assumed that Ben's death had occurred during the Barclays' party or soon after, though why he should go out in the dark nobody could explain. The remains of a glass of beer, a half-peeled apple and a tin of mushroom pâté added to the mystery. Everyone was as puzzled as Charlotte had been by the pâté, which it seemed unlikely that Jeff or Vicky would have given him. They would have heard about Ben's death by now as Mrs

Wolfe, who had their London telephone number in her caretaking capacity, would have relished telling them all the facts, both true and embroidered.

The paper was dry enough now. Loading her brush with thick white gouache from a tube, Rosemary skimmed it over the rough surface to lighten the creeks and pools. She dipped her brush into water and watched the strings of white paint curl into the liquid before she rattled the brush clean against the sides of the jar. As she flicked the water away on to the grass, she noticed two people dawdling on the old sluice-gate that once controlled the water in and out of the creek. They moved together and became one shape as they embraced, but they were too far off for Rosemary to recognise.

She returned to her painting but found her mind wandering back to Ben again and again. His cottage was in a worse state that anyone could have imagined. Her only comfort was that he wouldn't have been happy if anyone had tried to chivvy him into doing anything when he was alive.

Adrian Petherbridge had taken it upon himself to deal with the inquest and the funeral arrangements. His wife Carol had put up a determined show of possessiveness, informing Rosemary that she would sort through the contents of Ben's cottage and clean it. Rosemary had been emphatic that the job could not be done by one person and said that she and Charlotte would help.

The information that there was a daughter in Rington, although she hadn't been on speaking terms with the old man for years, came from Mrs Wolfe. She also mentioned Hilda Wilkins suffered badly from arthritis and couldn't get about much.

Rosemary had offered to drive over to Rington that morning to tell her the sad news. The painting, which was a quick watercolour sketch, was being undertaken as a calming-down exercise. She would pack up soon so that she could get back in time to prepare Peter and Kate's breakfast.

She became aware that the couple were below her now on the road in front of the creek. The lanky boy had his arm about the girl's shoulders with his cheek nuzzling the top of her head. He stopped to push back her long hair and, lowering his head, gave her an extended kiss. Rosemary knew them both and expected that they would feel awkward when they saw her. Slowly the girl moved away to look at her.

'Hello.' Kate waved one hand. 'What a great morning.'

Colin, who had not noticed Rosemary on the sea-wall, turned to glower at her.

Rosemary drove inland beside a field of pale blue flax that stretched like a sea into the distance. At Rington, she parked her car in the road outside Hilda Wilkins's bungalow. The bricks were hidden under porridge-coloured rendering. A deeply pitched roof of slates partly obscured two sash windows at the front, like a dark grey helmet pulled over a pair of eyes.

After a search, Rosemary came across the only door in the wooden extension at the back of the house. She banged with her hand as there appeared to be nothing to knock or press.

Hilda was so long answering that Rosemary had decided she must be out when she heard a scuffling inside and the door scraped back over a coconut mat, revealing a woman leaning over her stick. She was small and round and her pale eyes had the look of a dog anxious to please. Her chin and her upper lip were short and flat after many years of shrinking over false teeth. She wore a floral wraparound pinafore, sleeveless and tied at the back, strained around her plump body.

'Mrs Wilkins?' Rosemary asked.

She nodded with a smile revealing dentures as yellow as toasted almonds.

'I'm Rosemary Lawrence. Would it be convenient for me to talk to you for a few minutes?'

The lids of Hilda's small eyes fluttered and her face reddened. 'Come along in then, Mrs Lawrence.'

The scullery had trapped the odour of years of over-cooked cabbage and fry-ups. Hilda dragged herself over a jigsaw of carpet-pieces and up a step into the living room.

'Can I get you a cuppa tea?' She reached the mantelpiece and rested her hand on it beside a line of cavorting pottery children. Despite the hot weather, an ashy fire glimmered in the grate, a fire, Rosemary suspected rightly, that was kept in all the year round. She declined the tea and sat down while Hilda tossed aside a cheap magazine before she lowered herself the short distance to a chair made high with cushions.

'It's me hip,' she whined apologetically. 'I'm waiting to be called in for the op.'

Rosemary soon discovered that all her anxiety about breaking the news of Ben's death was unnecessary because Adrian had called earlier. It had been agreed that Rosemary should do it and her first angry reaction was of a wasted journey, but then she was glad she had called, for although it was obvious sympathy was not required, Hilda was glad to have a visitor.

It seemed that Ben had alienated himself from the family a long time ago.

'Me and Bill hasn't kep' in touch with Dad for a good few years. Not since our mum died.' Shyly Hilda examined the roses on her pinafore. 'That's no good saying he weren't an awkward bugger, Mrs Lawrence, because he were. Bill couldn't abide Dad.'

Her neck grew red streaks as she feared she had said too much.

'Let me get you a cuppa tea, Mrs Lawrence,' she burst out. 'Won't take a minute for the old kettle to boil.' She began to rise from her chair.

'No, really, thank you.' Rosemary thought the preparations would be too irksome. 'I hear that Mr Petherbridge has offered to deal with everything.'

'Yes. Dad's to be buried with our mum. Mr Featherbridge will arrange it. He say we can't do nothing till after the post-mortem, decide the day of the funeral and that. I say

76

to Bill we ought to make a few paste sandwiches and have one or two of them back, but he won't hear of it. Shouting and swearing he was, Mrs Lawrence. "He done nothing for us," Bill say, "and we do nothing for him, alive or dead," he say.'

'Of course there's no need, people will understand.' Rosemary looked at the sideboard, where a meagre lamp-shade was balanced drunkenly on a thin wooden base, and changed the subject. 'I know it's a bit early to talk about such things, but while I'm here, what's going to happen to the contents of the cottage? There's no hurry and I don't want to interfere. Perhaps we should wait until after the funeral anyway. But can you manage, Mrs Wilkins? Have you any friends or relations to help you clear it and clean the place up?'

Hilda's eyes fluttered again at the enormity of the task.

'Bill say he'll get his mate, Duggy, to take us over some time to get a few things. But Bill won't touch the clearing and cleaning and that. I'm at my wits' end when I think on it for what can I do with this old hip, Mrs Lawrence?'

'You're not to worry. One or two of us from the village were fond of Ben. We'll rally round to help. We won't dispose of anything until you've seen it.'

'There's that clock,' said Hilda, losing her shyness with indignation. 'On the mantelpiece it was, oak and carved beautiful, all leaves and squirly bits. And a gold face, Mrs Lawrence.'

'It's still there. I saw it the other day.'

'Mum always say I could have it but Dad wouldn't listen. And that was poor old Mum's clock to give. Come from her side of the family, you see, Mrs Lawrence. Dad always say he would stamp it to pieces before he'd let me lay a finger on it. So I say to Bill, that's no good, is it? And Bill say he hope it fall off the mantelpiece and kill him. Wicked talk! He was all for going over there but he listened to me for once. He never go, Mrs Lawrence.'

'You'll be able to have your clock soon, Mrs Wilkins.'

'Bill reckon there won't be no will. Our mum never

left no will. If she had that clock would be in this house today.'

'I don't think you have anything to worry about. I'm sure your father didn't bother with a will. He told me as much.'

What Ben had actually said was, 'Let them squabble over me bits when I'm underground.'

Hilda's face relaxed. 'That's all right then. Now how about a nice cuppa tea?'

Adrian Petherbridge, seated at the table for lunch, demanded freshly made English mustard to go with the shepherd's pie Carol had made from the last of Sunday's beef.

'All right!' Carol slammed her napkin down. 'That's only yesterday's, Adrian. There's nothing wrong with it.'

He pushed the unacceptable pot away in a finicky manner. 'Mustard should be mixed anew for every meal,' he said, affecting the plummy voice he had perfected to conceal his East London background. He grinned with satisfaction at his small victory while he poured a glass of home-made blackcurrant syrup and held it up to the light as if it were the rarest burgundy.

'The colour's good,' he called.

'Can't hear,' Carol shouted untruthfully from her immaculate kitchen. The cupboards were white-fronted and the white work-tops were as hygienic and uncluttered as a deserted operating theatre. All the dirty utensils had been washed and hidden away before the meal started. Only the microwave was allowed space as it blinked the time in apologetic green digits.

Carol returned, stirring the mustard briskly. While he rolled a little of the purple liquid round his mouth Adrian sniffed the bouquet.

'It needs to be,' he smacked his lips together, 'a little less cold. Too much chilling impairs the flavour.'

'Would you like me to heat it up for you, dear?'

'I think not, dear. Shall I pour you a glass? It's fortunate that little subtleties like incorrect temperature don't bother you.'

'I prefer uncontaminated spring water with my lunch.'

'This blackcurrant syrup could take its place unashamedly beside any wine you could mention. It does contain brandy, you know.'

'So does brandy butter.'

Carol pushed a mouthful of shepherd's pie into her mouth to hide a smile. Although neither would admit it, they enjoyed the abrasive point-scoring that resembled a double act at a music hall. The skirmish over, they resumed a more profitable conversation.

'You'll be pleased to hear I'm keeping an eye on all Ben Pearce's affairs, dear. Once the post-mortem is carried out and the coroner issues the burial order, I shall deal with the funeral.'

'Yes, dear.'

'Of course there'll be an inquest as the old man was drowned but we won't hear the result of that for a few weeks.'

'I see.'

'That little Wilkins woman seems relieved that I'm dealing with everything. And I've also bought some rolls of chicken wire and nets.'

'Our garden is like a fortress already, Adrian!'

'Not for us, dear, for Vicky Barclay. Her garden is over-run with rabbits and she beseeched me to erect some kind of barricade to keep them out.'

'She doesn't grow anything worth protecting.'

'She seems to dote on her roses. We can't have the destructive little creatures nibbling at the shoots.'

'Just like her to get you running around after her. I hope she's paying for it.'

'I have the receipt.' He rose from the table so that he could produce it from his wallet. 'And what are you doing this afternoon, dear?'

'I'm leading the ponies at the riding-stables. It's the handicapped children's monthly visit.'

'So it is. I had forgotten. I shall make a start on the Barclays' garden. It'll be a nice surprise for them when they come again.'

Carol drank her coffee as she washed up, to save time. She was continually analysing her week to make certain that she was using it to best advantage. So that her flare for organising should not be wasted, she ran jumble sales and helped arrange fêtes for the church and sat on committees to raise money for charitable causes. She collected pensions for the housebound and visited people who were off-colour and terminally ill.

Once or twice she had considered taking up Rosemary's offer to paint with her but she wasn't over-keen. It was bad for her confidence to share an activity when she was the amateur. In the autumn, she thought, she might go to evening classes in Lynn – something academic, perhaps, like Italian lessons. She had always been fascinated by the sound of that language, especially the rhythmical way the words were pronounced. '*Ponti Vecchio*,' she said to a fork as she washed it.

It had been a pleasant surprise to find that life had not been as traumatic as she had imagined when Adrian had been given early retirement a year ago, at the age of fifty-five. He had not minded retiring. In fact he told everyone that the substantial golden handshake he had received denoted the contribution he had made to the company. He had no desire to uproot and move to Peterborough with the firm, which was the only other option.

Carol was nearly six years younger than Adrian and she knew she did not look her age. Humming to herself, she rinsed the tea towel and hung it on the line before she went in to change.

On the grass by the bridge the ducks were either too lethargic to stir or knew it was not worth exerting themselves for Adrian. They watched his slight figure trundling the wheelbarrow along the hot road and heard the mallet, a roll of chicken wire and other pieces of equipment rattle against the metal interior.

Carol was using the car and, although he had been noisy with indignation, Adrian appreciated that he could wheel the barrow straight into the Barclays' garden which was easier than unloading the stuff from the boot of the car.

Before starting work he jumped up and down on a line of molehills that ran across the grass to flatten them. Next he had an inquisitive peer over the Jackmanii. He noted with disgust Ben's outside privy before turning his eyes to the wilderness of lanky spinach going to seed. What a disgrace, he thought. People who could not control their gardens should be forced to sell them to those who could. Adrian's garden was controlled to the last blade of grass, except for a small triangle in one corner, where field poppies and mallow and wild grasses were left to scatter their seeds in the interests of conservation.

He caught the sound of faint music drifting from somewhere not far away. He could hear the thump of the bass and an occasional high note. It was not coming from Ben's cottage, which he had locked himself, and the Barclays were in London. He walked across to their kitchen window. The blind was half-drawn-up, making the sunlight into bars that fell over an empty can of Coke in the sink. He was sure the music was coming from somewhere inside. Then he remembered Mrs Wolfe. Of course, she would be cleaning up after the party. He knocked on the window, calling, 'Mrs Wolfe, can you hear me?' It was obvious she could not. He considered going round to the front door but changed his mind. She would recognise him if she saw him in the garden.

He went back to the wheelbarrow, lifted out the chicken wire and began to unroll it. When the job was complete and he was about to return home, he noticed that the house was silent and the kitchen blind had been pulled down.

After Rosemary had been taken into the Barclays' garden to admire Adrian's work, they walked back to Dilly's gate where he left her to go home. In her hand she carried a packet of washing-up powder that Dilly had absent-mindedly left on Betty Tiller's counter.

A glassed-in verandah ran the full length of the bungalow, with the main entrance in the centre. Through the open folding doors that divided the verandah from the two main rooms she caught a glimpse of Dilly moving about. Rosemary tapped the metal Welshwoman that formed the knocker. Dilly came, her tissue-paper face creased into a welcoming smile and her vest strap visible where the neckline of her dress had slipped down. She insisted that Rosemary came in and sat her in a Victorian armchair, which had been banished to the verandah because of its lumps, while a cup of tea was made for her. It was not long before Rosemary wriggled off the uncomfortable springs to inspect the pot-plants, where they stood on the dusty window-ledges surrounded by dry insect corpses. The pungent smell of geraniums clogged the air as they struggled to lift round leaves to the sun. They survived or withered depending on the frequency of the water that streamed over them from Dilly's watering-can.

The sound of bone-china cups rattling on their unmatching saucers preceded Dilly, who appeared holding a tray.

'I hope you don't mind odd china, each pretty in its own right. They do break easily, don't they!'

'They're very fragile,' agreed Rosemary.

'We'll miss old Ben, you know, dear.'

'Yes.' Rosemary took her tea and sat down quickly, avoiding the Victorian chair.

'Do have a biscuit,' said Dilly. 'We had nothing in common, mind. A house that has someone living in it has a comfortable look. These weekenders' places are like dogs waiting for their owners to return.'

'I know what you mean.' Rosemary ate a piece of biscuit that was soft like damp pastry.

'Rats!' Dilly flopped into a garden chair. 'Along Ben's hedge, you know. He told me he'd been bitten once. It went septic and he had to go to hospital. He set traps but they still bothered him. Proper nuisance they were. Not those in the traps, of course – the others.'

'Surely they don't attack us!' said Rosemary. 'Unless they're cornered.'

'Best take what Ben said with a pinch of salt. Old people do get these funny ideas, don't they?' She dunked her already soft biscuit into her tea. 'Ben preferred to see the enemy. He refused to go out in the dark, because of his rats.'

'He went out the night he died.'

'That's right, dear.' The biscuit lingered in the air for a second before Dilly chewed at a piece, leaving a dribble of tea on her chin.

Rosemary waited, hoping for some more revelations.

'Rats do go for ducks' eggs,' said Dilly. 'And the ducklings. Still, that's nature's way. We can't be overrun with them, can we, dear? Foxes do take them too, mind. The rascals are dab hands at tipping my dustbin over.'

'Do you think there was anything sinister about Ben's death, Dilly?'

'Did I say that, dear?'

'No. But you said he never went out in the dark.'

'That's right. It's sensible to stay in, isn't it? Especially if rats worry you.'

'He had an outside loo!'

'And an inside chamber-pot. I don't get on with those, do you, dear? Neither did Ben now that I come to think of it. He took advantage of his open bedroom window during the night. Watered the gravel, you know.' Suddenly Dilly put her cup and saucer on the ground and clasped her gnarled hands together. 'What an interesting man Kenneth Weaver is, don't you think? I took him to Snettisham Church on our little outing. I wish I could do brass-rubbing. There was a young girl in another church we visited doing black on gold, so pretty. But once I got down on those cold slabs, mind, I'd never get up again. Kenneth said why didn't I take a few photos instead. "Flash," he said. Do you know about flash?'

Rosemary nodded.

'Is it a bit too modern for me, do you think? I'm willing to have a go.'

'Oh no. These new cameras are easy to use.'

'His wife has gone abroad. Cat. Is that right?'

'I think so. I know very little really. Kenneth arrived with so much stuff I can't think how they've crammed it all in. The rooms must resemble a furniture store.'

'Fascinating!'

'As for that monster piano! I saw the men trying to get it through the front door. His wife plays, professionally, I mean. I think she's gone off on some sort of concert tour abroad.'

'How very exciting!' Dilly had pleasant recollections of musical evenings before the war when she thumped an accompaniment to her sister's reedy rendering of 'David of the White Rock'. 'When she comes back we must have a get-together. He's got a golden retriever called Tosca, after the opera, he said, and she lay like a sphinx in the back of the car when we were out.'

'Did you know he's gone away?' said Rosemary.

'No, dear, I'm sure you're wrong. He didn't say.'

'Yes. He called to tell me.'

Dilly was silent, the animation vanished from her face, making Rosemary wish she hadn't said anything. He might have mentioned that he was going, she thought.

'He must have left in a great hurry,' said Dilly. 'I've tried ringing him twice. Called away suddenly, see. Yes, that would be it, called away suddenly.'

Pressing her hands on the arms of her chair she rose stiffly and, reaching across to prod a finger on the rock-hard earth in a geranium pot, she decided it needed watering. While she was indoors Rosemary noticed Colin walking towards the verandah. He knocked and peered through the window. When he saw her his grin of expectation, an expression Rosemary was not familiar with, changed to one of displeasure. He stared at his feet as she opened the door.

'I've come to cut the grass,' he said, defiantly.

Dilly had heard his knock as she returned with a kettle of water. 'Come along in, Colin, lovely. Have you forgotten you cut it last Friday?'

'It needs doing again.'

'It hasn't grown much. We've had no rain, see. In fact

it's getting a bit on the brown side. I'm sure yours is the same, Rosemary.'

'Well – no, ours is rather long.'

'There's a job for you, then, lovely,' said Dilly cheerfully.

His reply was arrogant. 'I might do it later.'

Rosemary found herself murmuring that it would be nice if he could and said she must go as she promised to call on Charlotte, which she had not.

As she leaned on the parapet of the bridge, surrounded by ducks, she thought about her conversation with Dilly. Was it as exaggerated as Ben's had always been? Yet Dilly was no fool. She would not be unaware of the significance of her words. It was difficult to understand what she was getting at. And Colin, what an uncouth boy he was. Charlotte really didn't deserve him.

She glanced up at Ben's cottage. Dilly was right, it had a desolate appearance despite the fact that it had not been cleared of furniture. Ben had not been a happy man, yet in retrospect his sharp tongue and constant whingeing had had an odd charm.

Mrs Wolfe came along the road carrying a baby over one shoulder, calling, 'Ducks, ducks, look at the ducks, baby, look at the pretty ducks.' Making her way through their feathered bodies she reached Rosemary and told her in one breath that her daughter had left the baby in her charge while she went to Yarmouth for the day with her new boyfriend.

'Off she go on the back of that motorbike all dressed up in helmet and high heels and leather trousers and they great heavy metal earrings. "You'll drag your ear-lobes right down, mark my words," I say to her.'

While she was talking the baby turned his head to stare at Rosemary with protruding blue eyes and a crooked mouth, which she was flattered into thinking was a smile until his face took on a surprised expression. The baby belched.

'That's a beauty,' said Mrs Wolfe in a high singsong voice, screwing her head round to see him. 'He full of wind, Mrs Lawrence. It's all they solids babies are given these days. Two months is too young to start. My Jackie say I'm old-fashioned but his little stomach isn't up to it, is it my little lamb! And what's more, I say to her, I think a baby need a father, specially a boy.'

'I'm inclined to agree with you, Mrs Wolfe. But these young people are all the same.'

'Oh no, Mrs Lawrence. Take your Emma. She's lovely. You'll never have no trouble with your Emma.'

Rosemary wished she felt as confident.

'And how are you getting along with that other little girl?' said Mrs Wolfe. 'Irish, isn't she?'

'Kate? Oh, very well thank you.'

'Isn't she a little duck. And all that lovely goldy hair!'

She became aware that the baby had fallen asleep, his plump cheek flattened against her shoulder. She continued the remainder of the conversation in a stage whisper, saying she must get back to see if Mr Wolfe was home to look after his lordship so that she could give the Barclays' cottage a proper clean. She clucked and said she wondered what sort of state it would be in after the party.

Peter had come home early. The computer at work had failed when he was in the middle of writing a complicated program and it had been too late to get involved with anything else.

He reclined in an easy chair, looking through the French windows at the motionless trees in the garden. He always thought they attained their peak of beauty in July, before they began to change, imperceptibly at first, to overblown tiredness when August arrived.

Everything was quiet. Even the clock was silent. It had stopped at ten past three. Peter dragged himself up to reach for the key behind it. There was no point in having clocks around the place that weren't going. It was the carriage clock that Rosemary had bought him for some anniversary, their fifteenth probably, and the thought that she had certainly paid through the nose for it didn't spoil his pleasure. The clock started to tick in a fussy, comfortable way. He polished

86

the dial with his handkerchief and replaced it gently on the shelf before he sat down again.

The grass needed cutting, he'd have to tackle it himself if that boy of Charlotte's didn't buck up his ideas. How satisfying it would be to have a lawn ribbed pale and dark green. Some chance while Colin drove the mower but Peter would rather repair the machine than push it.

He caught sight of the television in the corner and remembered he had promised Rosemary he would have a look at it. Yesterday evening, when he had left the room, the picture on the screen had dissolved into crackling spots, only returning to the calm voice and head of the newsreader a few seconds before Peter came back again. Rosemary had complained.

'Nothing wrong now,' he had said.

'Call me a liar?'

'No, but look at it!'

'I was trying to!'

'Sorry, love. I believe you.'

'You'd better!'

He must examine it some time, not now, perhaps after supper. Also after supper he must try to discover what the knocking was at the back of the car. Two people were needed to identify it so if he could persuade Rosemary to drive he could listen from the back seat.

He wondered what Kate was up to. The house had been left open so he had no way of knowing if she was in her bedroom. She hadn't replied when he bellowed for Rosemary. Kate was a strange kid, always washing her hair. She was no trouble, almost demure, like some polite little convent-educated colleen. Pity Emma was away but Kate didn't seem to mind amusing herself. It was odd the way she had suddenly appeared in that white outfit. Even Peter, who rarely noticed what people wore, had thought she looked pretty good. He was used to Emma turning up in the most outrageous garb, not always to her enhancement. He made a rule never to comment on her clothes.

Rosemary came into the room wearing a home-made sundress.

'You're home early!'

'The computer packed up. You're lucky to have this all day.'

'Yes, but I don't sit around all day admiring it.' Rosemary sat down wearily to admire it now.

'Been out painting?'

'No. To Dilly's.' She kicked off her flip-flops. 'She's got some bee in her bonnet about Ben. Thinks he might have been pushed.'

Peter sat up, startled. 'What! That's ludicrous. Whatever put that absurd notion into her head?'

'Calm down. She's nothing to go on. I didn't take it seriously.'

'She's a stupid old woman. She mustn't go around spreading rumours like that. Think of the trouble it would cause.'

'Don't worry. She's not spreading it around,' said Rosemary. 'I meant to tell you, I saw Kate and Colin together, yesterday, when I was painting by the old harbour.'

'What were they up to?'

'Dangling round each other's necks. I got the impression that Colin was more smitten than Kate. Oh dear, Peter! How responsible are we for Kate? Supposing it were Emma. What would you do?'

'Colin's not a monster.'

'You know perfectly well what I mean. He's never going to earn his own living and although he's Charlotte's son, I do find it hard to like him. He's so aggressive! Would you have a word with Kate?'

'Why? It can't be serious. They've only just met, and I don't expect she'll be staying long.' Peter yawned sleepily. 'Sorry! Good luck to him, I say. I don't expect the poor kid's had much opportunity to have a girlfriend before.'

'Peter, you don't understand what I'm getting at.' Rosemary sighed. 'He's so ... so ... '

'Don't add a third complication. We do enough fussing about our own two offspring. As far as I can see, Colin is harmless and Kate's not staying for ever.'

'And that's another thing. How long *is* she staying? I

don't mind all that much but is she going to wait until Emma gets back?'

'I expect that's the general idea. I think it's nice to have someone young about the place.'

'She's inclined to borrow things without asking. Emma's bike, for instance.'

'We probably weren't there to ask. Emma won't mind.'

Neither of them spoke for a minute. Outside in the lush foliage, a ring dove began to croon its plaintive call again and again.

'Peter?' said Rosemary.

'Yes, love.'

'You won't be offended if I ask you something?'

'Depends. I shouldn't think so.'

'Do you think Kate's attractive?'

'Yes. She's a pretty child. Gorgeous eyes and hair.' He waited. 'Was that it?'

'Not exactly. I mean more than that.' Rosemary felt her cheeks reddening. 'Do you find her . . . beddable?'

'What a quaint way of putting it. Beddable! I can honestly say it's never entered my head. Charlotte now . . . '

'Be serious, Peter. Has Kate ever made a pass at you?'

'Good grief, love, you're not serious! She's an innocent! I've always found her very proper,' he said. 'Thanks for your vote of no-confidence.'

'Sorry, darling. I just feel . . . I don't know.'

Peter put on a mock whining voice. 'That's not to say I'm a middle-aged has-been.'

Rosemary gave up. The conversation had taken a flippant turn so it was useless to continue. She believed Peter absolutely.

'I'd be glad if you'd give me a hand helping me to locate a knock in the car,' Peter said. 'After supper. Anything to eat? I'm hungry.'

11

Colin sat on the window-ledge in his bedroom with the sash up, watching a lapwing flap slowly over the honey-coloured wheatfield that separated his house from the salt-marsh. His mother came into the room carrying some freshly ironed shirts on her arm.

'Oh lovey, this room is a tip!' she said. 'Couldn't you tidy it up a bit?'

'No.' Sulkily Colin twisted the ring on his binoculars to focus them.

'Well, some time then.' Patiently, Charlotte hung the shirts in the wardrobe. 'You must have a good turn-out some time. What's that great metal dish thing in the corner there?'

'That's to amplify birdsong if you must know,' said Colin. 'And don't you dare move anything. This is my room.'

'Yes, lovey.' Because of his concentration he wasn't aware that she had taken several tapes off the bed and given the duvet a twitch to straighten it.

'What are you looking at?' she said.

'A lapwing. Want to see it?'

'Yes.' Through the lenses she saw a patchy fog of colour.

'Is the focus right? Turn the top,' Colin said. 'Got it?'

'Oh yes,' she said, pretending success. 'Super! Is it unusual?'

'No, they're here all the time.' He watched the bird glide slowly across the wheat, uttering its nasal call.

'Want me to play that froggy video game with you?' Charlotte asked.

'No thanks. You're useless at it. I want to tape some notes about the lapwing's behaviour when you've gone.'

After she had closed the door he switched on the machine and began to talk into it.

Downstairs Charlotte found Kate waiting, standing in the middle of the hall.

'Hello, lovey. Have you been here long?'

'No.' Kate's smile was charming. 'It's Colin I've come to see.'

'He's upstairs playing with his tape thingy. He might like you to play Leaps, it's one of those computer games with frogs jumping all over the place. You'll be better than me. My reactions are a bit slow and Colin gets annoyed.'

'Yes,' said Kate. 'I'm wanting to hear the tapes.'

'Up you go then.'

Leaning against the curtains Charlotte lit a cigarette. She opened her mouth an inch, letting a coil of smoke trickle out, and wondered if the fabric reeked and if other people found it objectionable. She was never conscious of it herself but perhaps she ought to get the curtains cleaned some time. Another thing she must do was clean the car. It was a task she rarely bothered about but since hooligan fingers had scraped words on the dusty boot and doors when she was in the bank last week, it had to be done. She stubbed out the cigarette, squirted washing-up liquid into a bucket of water and took it outside.

She had parked the car at the front in the shadow of the house because even with the windows open it became an inferno in the sun. She glanced up at Colin's bedroom. This girlfriend situation was a new, delightful experience for her. Kate was so pretty and unassuming.

The sponge released a river of white bubbles as she swept it across the bonnet. Thoughts that had never entered her head before began to creep in. After all, why not, Colin was not physically unattractive! She had to admit that he had an abrupt manner but that could be put down to shyness and it hadn't deterred Kate so far.

On the drive the water dripped into frothy pools around the edges of the car, wetting Charlotte's bare feet and the hem of her long black shift.

Colin would have the house and enough money to keep it going with careful investment by the accountant. She stopped to look at the exterior. It was large and could be split into two dwellings with the addition of a small extension, which could include a second kitchen and bathroom, so that she could be completely independent while they lived in the main part. She wouldn't mind that.

She walked round the car tossing water over the four wheels and returned indoors to refill the bucket. As she stepped through the French windows she heard the heavy thudding of feet coming down the stairs. Someone tried to open the front door, unsuccessfully because of the bolts.

'You can't get out that way,' Colin said. 'Kate, come back.'

In the hall Kate whispered, 'Hush, she'll hear you.'

'It's all right. She's outside washing the car,' Colin replied. 'Come upstairs again. *Please!*'

'I'm not trusting you, Colin Franklin,' said Kate, coyly.

'It won't happen again.'

'It had better not. Promise now.'

'I promise.'

'You're a desperate terror.' Her voice was provocative. 'Do you know that?'

'Be kind to me, Kate, and no one will ever know,' said Colin.

'I will, I will, just give me time,' said Kate. 'I get scared.'

No sound came from the hall for a minute. Charlotte was aware that she was behaving shamefully but she dared not move.

'I love you,' said Colin, in a tone Charlotte had never heard before.

'Behave yourself now, Colin Franklin,' Kate said primly.

'I will if you come upstairs again. Please, Kate.'

'I just might then.'

'And I'll play some bird tapes for you.'

'Great. Better than that old frog game.'

Charlotte rattled the handle of the bucket and stamped her feet to pretend she was just entering the house. She heard them go upstairs.

Colin trying to get his wicked way with Kate! Good grief! She was astounded. But she had no intention of interfering.

Returning to the car with a full bucket, Charlotte smiled to herself. Colin's old swing was in the garage and she'd kept several of his toys and books. She remembered how he used to run about shouting 'Stop fief', imitating Mr McSomebody after she'd read him Peter Rabbit. It was strange that he had turned against reading.

A mallard quacked, making her jump as it flapped its wings, scattering water from a puddle that had formed around one of the car wheels.

12

The post-mortem examination on Ben Pearce had finally been carried out. Adrian had collected the burial order and made arrangements for the funeral which was to take place the following day. He walked beside a ragged line of holly-hocks that raised their pale yellow flowers high above Dilly's hedge and congratulated himself on efficiently completing all the arrangements for the funeral tomorrow.

He opened the gate to deliver a bunch of home-grown radishes that he had washed clean as cherries and shorn of their trailing roots before binding them neatly together with an elastic band. He knocked on Dilly's door and wandered off inquisitively without waiting for an answer. An expression of disfavour crossed his face as he toured the gloriously rampant flower-beds. Behind the unpruned roses, bindweed twisted through shoulder-high nettles. Trumpet flowers and fat pointed buds shone white out of the dense leaves. Adrian saw a rabbit disappear into a tangle of honeysuckle. He turned quickly away.

He paused at a long garden seat built of planks, which had been pushed against the side of the bungalow. The wooden boards had split in the centre and rust had broken through the curved metal ends. The whole seat was spattered white, fouled by perching birds.

'Cooee, hello.' Dilly leaned from the doorstep. 'Anyone there?'

'Here,' shouted Adrian without moving, so that Dilly was forced to come to him. 'My dear Mrs Harris, what an appalling waste!'

'What's that, Mr Petherbridge?'

'This could be an excellent seat.' He pushed the radishes into her hand without an explanation so that she got the impression that she was holding them for him. Then he lowered his finger on to a broken plank between two splashes of bird-lime and pushed to test its strength.

'That seat's not as young as it was,' said Dilly. 'Like me.'

A large blackberry bush pressed against the wall. After rubbing his finger with a handkerchief he flung out his hand in a bold gesture.

'If that were drastically cut back, the seat could go centrally along there.'

'But the blackberries,' said Dilly. 'What would I put in my jelly?'

'That seat's far too valuable to rot away.'

'But I can't sit on it, see,' said Dilly, patiently. 'Last time I did it cracked. D'you see? Under by there?'

'That's what I'm saying,' snapped Adrian.

'A cushion might help if you think it's uncomfortable,' said Dilly, turning towards the bungalow to fetch one.

'Oh, no,' said Adrian, regretting his impoliteness. 'You see, old ladies mustn't take risks.'

'I'm not expecting any old ladies to sit on it.' She placed the washed radishes on the seat.

Adrian crumpled his face so that his eyes closed. 'I suppose you wouldn't have a Paracetamol?'

'Oh, poor man. Feeling under the weather, is it?'

'My head is splitting. I really should be in bed.'

'You're welcome to have a lie-down on my sofa.'

Adrian ignored this. He said he was exhausted after dealing with all Ben Pearce's arrangements. That morning he'd taken Hilda Wilkins to the florist to see about her flowers and after that he'd spent time digging up some of the spinach in Ben's garden.

'And not a word of thanks from anyone.'

'Well, I hope you weren't expecting any from Ben,' said Dilly. 'Of course you do know he's being buried tomorrow?'

'I know more about Ben's affairs than anyone,' said

95

Adrian. 'All the queries and the problems have been settled by me alone. I've tied up all the loose ends.'

'Very creditable,' said Dilly bending to pull at a stubborn dandelion. 'We all have to go some time. Not a bit of good worrying about the inevitable. Won't you come in?'

'No, it's time I went home.' When he reached the gate he shouted, 'I'll get hold of a piece of wood for that seat.'

'Don't trouble yourself about that, Mr Petherbridge,' called Dilly. 'I bring a folding chair out when I need one, see. Much more comfortable.'

'When I can I'll see to it and I'll get Carol to run you up a few bright cushions.'

Indoors Dilly found some aspirins at last and laughed to herself when she remembered why she had looked for them. The bottle was empty anyway. She was in a light-hearted mood. Kenneth had phoned to apologise for leaving without telling her. She had told him about Ben and they had had quite a chat.

Later that day she discovered the bundle of radishes lying on the seat. What a shame Mr Petherbridge had forgotten them. They were beautiful radishes.

On the morning of Ben's funeral the weather changed. There had been rain in the night and the hearse drew slowly away from his cottage in a blustery shower that rocked the long, damp nettles on the verges.

The mourners barely filled the two front pews of the large wool church and, in the chancel, the coffin stood isolated, looking too insignificant to be the reason for the gathering. Rosemary glanced around her. She knew everyone there. Peter and Dilly beside her, Adrian and Carol in front, next to Hilda, watchful and prepared in case she needed comforting. A little apart from them, Bill Wilkins was glowering in a hairy, ill-fitting suit. Charlotte and Leonard Graham stood together. The mushroom farmer was only there because he felt that he was an important part of the proceedings as his son had found the body. Across the aisle Mrs Wolfe pressed a white handkerchief to her nose. A little crowd of people from the village, who found attending funerals as compulsive as attending weddings, sat at the back of the nave more curious than sympathetic.

After the service they all followed the coffin, walking over a narrow strip that had been cut through the grass to form a path leading to the graveyard at the rear of the church. A wreath of red roses and Gypsophila trembled on top of the coffin as the bearers jolted it along. The rain had stopped. As they walked under a holm oak a gust of wind pushed large drops of water off the glossy leaves on to Rosemary's hair. They passed a litter-bin stuffed with dying flowers.

When they came to the graves Rosemary could not help noticing how varied they were. A flower-pot containing red Begonias stood at the base of a small, wooden cross blackened by the weather. Nearby, a large florid headstone was carved into garlands of marble roses and leaves surrounding the name of a recently dead publican, with a space below where his wife's name would be inscribed one day. On the grave she had lovingly arranged apricot roses in a matching vase. All caring people, thought Rosemary. How long would it be before Ben's plot was a forgotten hump of grass like several others? Pol's only ornament was a glass dome, damp with rain outside and condensation within, obscuring three greying plastic lilies. It had been moved to a mound of newly dug earth that was hidden under a strip of artificial turf.

Hilda was taken by the elbows as Carol and Adrian propelled her to the edge so that she could watch the coffin lowered on white tapes, while her husband remained where he was, sour and brooding at the base of the mound. He had put a check cap on his small head. The rest of the party positioned themselves round the trench. The church clock struck the hour and the rain came again with gusts of wind that overturned jam-jars of flowers and rustled the trees. The vicar's cassock flapped against his legs as he intoned the committal in a flat voice.

'Man that is born of a woman hath but a short time to live – ' It was barely audible. The wind blew back the brim of Hilda's straw hat, tugging her cheap chiffon scarf into a black flag. Carol released her arm to put up an umbrella that needed all her strength to hold it steady above Hilda.

When it was all over the rain stopped as suddenly as it had begun. The mourners started saying goodbye to Hilda and, as there was no invitation back for sherry and sandwiches, drifted away. Peter went back to work.

Rosemary bent over the flowers, looking for their spray, while beside her Charlotte pulled at the hem of her long skirt, which clung stickily to her legs.

'Ben's the only one of us who stayed dry,' she whispered.

'You are a shocker!'

'I know.'

Rosemary pointed to a spray of golden lilies. 'That one's ours.'

'Very nice,' said Charlotte. 'I should have sent one but the florist had closed when I rang. Never mind!'

The wreath of red roses and Gypsophila, that had been chosen with strict guidance from Adrian, was Hilda's, although a bow of gaudy yellow ribbon, stamped with the word 'Remembrance' at regular intervals, was entirely Hilda's idea. She had added Bill's name to the card because it seemed the done thing and, as it was written without his permission she hoped he would never find out.

There was a small basket of freesias and carnations shrouded in plastic film from Adrian and Carol, a mixed spray from Dilly and a costly arrangement from the Barclays.

The largest tribute lay at the end of the row. Pale yellow chrysanthemums interspersed with mauve statice had been arranged in the form of a cross. Rosemary read out the words on the card: 'Bless you. Sleep well. Much love, Katherine.'

'Who?' said Charlotte.

'Katherine.'

'Who's she?'

'I haven't a clue. Whoever she is, she wasn't here, was she? We'd have noticed someone strange.'

'A bit of Ben's murky past. The crafty old devil!'

As they walked back through the disused part of the churchyard their shoes became increasingly heavy with mud.

Fingers of ivy crept from under the hedge nearly smothering the path in places. When they reached the shorn grass a thrush, head tilted and motionless, suddenly stabbed its beak into the soft earth and dragged out a worm.

'Come back for some coffee,' said Charlotte. 'It'll cheer us up.'

PART FOUR

13

Early one Saturday morning after the inquest, when the death certificate had been issued at last, Ben's cottage was noisy with people inside and out. Carol tore a sack-coloured net curtain from the kitchen window and pushed it into a dustbin-liner with hands encased in plastic gloves. She shuddered.

The sink bore a coating of iron-grey sludge mingled with tea-leaves. Dry splashes covered the doors of a low cupboard, where unwashed milk bottles, emitting a sour smell, open cans and a few coupons from cereal packets that Ben had been collecting for some free gift, littered its lino top.

Carol didn't know where to start. There was only a cold-water tap which meant that she would have to heat every drop for cleaning. Impatiently she grabbed the kettle by a handle that was crudely fixed at one end by a bolt. It looked lethal. When it was filled she discovered that only one of the electric rings on the cooker was working and that was so coated with burnt food that it gave off a trickle of throat-catching smoke as it heated up. Quickly she placed the kettle on the ring. She looked about the squalid kitchen, feeling disgust instead of any satisfaction she might have expected from this act of charity.

It would have been more sensible to have stuck out for the front bedroom which Rosemary and Charlotte had chosen to clear. The stench had given her a headache already. She went outside for a gasp of fresh air but even that was contaminated by the privy close by.

'Given up already, dear?' Adrian dug in a brown cauliflower head with a sharp laugh.

'You can talk, Adrian, when you refuse to come inside the place.'

'Unfortunately I can't dig from inside.'

'You don't have to dig. There's enough to do in here for all of us.'

'I prefer digging to standing around doing nothing.'

This remark meant that Carol could not go in immediately. She folded her arms and although she could hear the steam huffing in the kitchen, she said, 'I'm waiting for the kettle to boil.'

Adrian stopped digging. 'Jolly good. I could do with a cup of coffee.'

'Bad luck then,' said Carol. 'You'll have to be satisfied with cold water out of a mucky cup as I need the hot for cleaning.'

Peter came round the corner of the cottage, screwdriver protruding from his shirt pocket. Carol smiled brightly to hide the embarrassment she felt, knowing he had probably overheard their conversation. He had been delegated to fetch the bedding downstairs so that Hilda could make a decision about what was to be done with it. Adrian was to drive over to fetch her later.

'Hello, you two. How's things?' Peter went inside quickly.

Five minutes later, Carol was staring at one hundred and nine jam-jars wedged together on a pantry shelf. She couldn't understand why anyone would want to hoard so many. It wasn't as if Ben made jam. She removed one, allowing the two behind to roll and crash to the floor.

'Well done,' called Adrian from outside.

Mixed with the broken glass Carol saw thirty-five pound coins.

In the front bedroom, damp fed the bubble growth that lifted the wallpaper beneath the window. The cheap furniture, so polished when Pol was alive, held dust like the coating of white powder she had flapped over her florid complexion. The air smelled of unwashed clothes.

As Rosemary slid the window up carefully because she

had noticed that one sash cord was broken, a grey cobweb stretched and snapped. She removed her hands slowly, relieved that the frame did not crash down.

'Ought I to prop it with something?'

'It'll be all right.' Charlotte was accustomed to such dilapidation in her own house.

'Fantastic!' said Rosemary. 'I wouldn't mind painting the view.'

Charlotte looked out at the wheatfield that reached to the sea-wall like a sandy desert. 'It's the same from Colin's room. Except for the gaggle of ducks or whatever you call them.'

'I think that's geese.'

The mallards lolled on the grass waiting for anything of interest to stir them. Ben's neat privet hedge partly obscured the holly-red Porsche that reflected shafts of dazzle from the sun on its gleaming chassis.

'That car is obscene,' said Rosemary.

'Lucky for some,' said Charlotte. 'I wonder why Ben didn't sleep in this room? It's better than the other one.'

'I don't expect he fancied it if Pol died in here.'

They swept up most of the dust and used rags to twist away the cobwebs entangled with the husks of insects that hung from the walls and ceiling. Then they agreed to make a start on the chest of draws, leaving the bed for Peter, who, although they were not aware of it, had been diverted and was lying on the floor in the living room repairing a lethal electric socket.

'Right,' said Charlotte.

'Anything of value on top,' said Rosemary. 'Any obvious rubbish in this plastic bag.'

The lowest drawer had not been touched since Pol died. It contained sheets, lovingly laundered, the folded edges pale grey from years of blown dust. Jumpers, vests and rolled stockings, crushed together in the centre drawer, were interspersed with tablets of cracked soap, barely perfumed now.

Charlotte stretched the elastic of a pair of Directoire knickers across her waist and waggled her ample hips

'Even fits me!'

'Go on. You've lost weight.'

'Lovey, you're a good friend, but I think you're right.'

One of the half-width drawers at the top seemed to have been churned about by Ben's hand. They pulled out newspaper cuttings, yellow with age, an unwashed sock and several pieces of butterscotch, sugary and soft in their wrappings, clinging to loose playing cards. The other drawer was partly jammed by a pile of Christmas cards tied with thread, a heap of church magazines and a photograph folded in tissue paper lying between them.

Charlotte unwrapped it carefully. 'It's Pol. I remember her like that.'

'Not a bad photograph. I wonder who took it?'

Pol was looking away from the camera, her plump contours highlighted by sunshine falling on one side of her face.

'Look,' groaned Charlotte. 'She's wearing that ghastly frog pendant I gave her. Dear old Pol. She was a good sort.'

'I expect Hilda would like that.' Rosemary put the photograph on the bed and disposed of the cards and magazines.

'Anything else?' said Charlotte.

'Only an old envelope.'

'Don't say we've found Ben's hidden millions at last!'

'There's something written on it in pencil. It's a bit faint.'

'What does it say?'

'Katherine.' Rosemary unstuck the flap and pulled out a curl of fine baby hair.

Behind closed curtains Jeff Barclay turned over in bed, pulling the duvet from Vicky's sprawling body.

'Good grief,' he moaned. 'I thought we bought this place for a bit of peace.'

'Brute. You woke me up.' Vicky tucked her long brown legs and arms into her naked body like a foetus.

'Listen to that row out there. Has that old fool come back to haunt us!'

'Not funny, Jeff.'

He went to the window to draw back the curtain. Over the fence he saw the upper part of Adrian jerking as he dug out Ben's vegetables.

'It's that Petherbridge guy. He's talking to someone.'

Suddenly it occurred to him that another person might have got in first with a bid for Ben's cottage. He'd better get moving.

Vicky reached out a hand to feel for her watch on the small round bedside table that was covered by a floor-length cloth of Laura Ashley fabric.

'Gosh, it's ten past ten.'

'What's the panic, sweetheart? We got here in the middle of the night, at least it seemed like it.' He gave a noisy yawn. 'Look at that diabolical netting all over our flower-beds. Haven't you cleared it off yet?'

'It would only offend Adrian. He imagines he's protecting us from fiendish rabbits.'

'The man's a nut-case.'

'I hope there aren't any trapped rabbits.'

'No chance. They're too smart.'

Vicky eyed Jeff's back. 'Put something on or he'll see you, darling.'

'So what! If he sees more than he's got himself he can throw his hat at it.' He was quoting one of his father's inexplicable expressions.

Vicky laughed as she got out of bed. Swiftly she took Jeff's white towelling bath-robe off the hook on the door and put it on, belting it tightly round the waist.

'Want me to find out for you?' she said.

'You cheeky bitch. You must be desperate.'

As she ran downstairs, folding back the long sleeves, she could hear Jeff shouting, 'I'll see about you later, madam.'

She went into the kitchen. It was more up-to-date than their London one and she'd better start badgering Jeff into spending a bit of money on a really luxurious replacement there, before he got involved with doing up Ben's cottage. That was going to cost a packet.

As she was drinking a glass of orange juice from the fridge her fingers touched something hard in the pocket of Jeff's bath-robe. She pulled out a tortoiseshell and diamanté hairclip. The last time she'd seen one like that had been in that Irish girl's hair at the party.

'Katherine!' said Charlotte. 'She's the one who sent those flowers.'

'She must be some sort of relation.'

'Yes. No surprise really,' said Charlotte. 'Pity. I was hoping Ben had some secret love-life.'

'At his age! You are a twit.'

'Let's ask Hilda who she is.' Charlotte returned the hair to the envelope and tucked it in her pocket. 'We'd better get all this other stuff downstairs for her to sort over.'

Peter looked round the door.

'I thought you were going to be here ages ago,' said Rosemary.

'I know, I know. The place is alive downstairs with bare wires. It's a wonder the old boy didn't electrocute himself. I've just done a bodge on two sockets.'

'Come and repair some of mine any time you like,' said Charlotte. 'Mr Puss chewed through the lamp flex when he was a kitten.'

Peter covered his eyes in mock dismay before he opened his hand.

'Look what I found downstairs on the mantelpiece. He unrolled a screw of newspaper. Inside was the frog pendant.

'Help, the wretched thing's come back to haunt me,' said Charlotte. 'Give it to Hilda, *please!*'

'No, Ben wanted someone else to have it,' said Peter.

'Who?'

Peter smoothed out the newspaper. 'Look. He's written "for Katherine" in the margin.'

No one had found time to clean the room downstairs and, to add to the original disorder, the table had been piled high with cardboard boxes and a rolled-up candlewick bedspread.

Bill arrived followed by Adrian and Carol, who were shouting abrupt instructions to each other over the head of Hilda as they hauled her in like a large doll.

'Careful, Adrian.'

'Mind her foot, Carol.'

'Take her stick then.'

'Move that pillow on the chair. Oh, I'll do it.'

'*Not* on the floor, Adrian, it's filthy.'

'So's the pillow, dear.'

Hilda would have been glad of the pillow, no matter how dirty, to make the seat of the chair higher. She was shaken painfully down while Bill watched without speaking. He leaned against the doorjamb, one small foot tucked behind the other.

'Thanks both,' Hilda raised a flushed face. 'I'd be jumping around if it wasn't for this old hip, Mrs Featherbridge.'

'I'll just pop the kettle on and we'll have some coffee,' said Carol, who'd brought a pint of milk, a tin of instant coffee and a germ-free spoon in a basket. 'I hope you don't mind decaffeinated. My husband won't drink any other.'

They could hear Charlotte descending the narrow treads of the staircase sideways and carefully as the three folded blankets she grasped obscured her feet.

'Hello, Mrs Wilkins,' she said, her head forced back and her chin embedded in damp wool. 'Adrian, be a dear and clear a space on the table for me.'

Rosemary followed, bumping a large plastic bag behind her. They heard Peter shout from the top, 'Why don't we chuck the lot down to the bottom? They couldn't be more disgusting.'

'Mr and Mrs Wilkins are here, Peter,' Rosemary called back.

Hilda eyed the blankets. 'I don't know how we'll wash that lot. They're not all that clean, are they, Bill?'

He ignored her.

Rosemary was surprised that this little man, who she had seen only once before at the funeral and who was quoted by Hilda on all matters, was so silent. Bars of grey hair had been combed across his balding head. His white bristly chin was unshaven as a defiant gesture, she was certain, and his jet eyes had a perceptible squint. They moved constantly from one person to another as he assessed whether or not he and Hilda were being cheated.

'This candlewick will wash well,' said Carol. 'Adrian will take anything you like to the launderette in Hunston, won't you, dear?'

'Yes, dear.' He would have preferred to have volunteered himself. 'You'll pack them all in plastic bags first, won't you, dear?'

'Would you like the blankets when they're washed, Mrs Wilkins?' asked Rosemary.

'Yes.' Her neck was scarlet. 'If they got a bit of warmth left in them.'

They discussed the furniture they could see.

'We got a rented telly,' said Hilda, 'so we won't want Dad's.'

'Course we'll have that,' interrupted Bill. ' 'Stead of renting our one. Use your loaf, Mother.'

Rosemary was startled by the low voice which was louder than she would have thought possible from such a little man.

'Bill say we'll be taking that then.' said Hilda.

'I think it's rented too,' said Charlotte.

Carol appeared with coffee in various well-washed cups and mugs that she had found behind the jam-jars.

'We'll have all this lot, Mother.' Bill reached over to poke dirt-engrained fingers through the handle of the largest mug.

'There's a reasonable chest of drawers upstairs,' said Rosemary.

'And I don't know what you'll think about the bed,' said Peter. 'It's not at all bad. I could unscrew it and get it downstairs somehow for you to see.' His eyes glowed at the challenge.

Bill slurped his coffee. 'Nothing wrong with my legs, mister.'

110

'Well no, of course not,' said Peter. 'Sorry! Do go up.'

'I will when I'm good and ready.'

'There are lots of odds and ends belonging to your mother, Hilda,' said Charlotte.

'We'll bring them down so that you can sort them through,' said Rosemary, glaring at Bill, determined that Hilda would not be thwarted. His black eyes wobbled and he looked away.

Charlotte pulled the envelope out of her pocket. 'Look what we found in the drawer upstairs.'

'Oh yes.' Hilda showed polite interest.

The curl of hair slid into Charlotte's hand. 'Look, it must have been cut from a baby.'

'Well I never. Who do that belong to then?'

'We don't want any old sentimental rubbish, Mother.' Bill tugged down the lovingly knitted cardigan that hung straight to his hips without touching them. 'Best burn the lot.'

'It seems to have belonged to Katherine,' said Charlotte.

For a minute Hilda said nothing. Then she pushed up her short chin and lifted her eyes to stop the tears running down. 'Joanie were our daughter. She's dead now though her hubby never say till she's been buried a year. It was all right when they was first married. "Mum," she say. "Mum, he's not a bad chap." Only Bill couldn't stand him.'

Bill interrupted from the doorway. 'She were dead to us, Mother, long before he bury her.'

Unexpectedly Hilda raised her voice. 'You chase them away, Bill Wilkins. That was terrible things you say to them. Terrible things! You go on and on, even now, to this day.'

'They was never welcome at ours,' muttered Bill. 'Never. Never will be.'

Hurriedly Carol began to collect the empty cups and mugs, smiling widely in her embarrassment. Everyone co-operated with exaggerated gestures. As she took Bill's mug she caught a whiff of unwashed flesh.

'Thought he was Lord Muck,' Bill shouted at Hilda. 'We

don't want his sort round here. I hope he die a slow lingering death.'

Carol gasped.

'Bill.' Hilda was sobbing. 'She were a good girl and our only one.'

'Stubborn. Your dad to a tee, that girl. Come on, Mother. We been here long enough, too long.'

He did not move away from the door, his eyes darting about the room, then, suddenly, he left.

Charlotte put her arm around Hilda as she comforted her. 'Don't distress yourself.'

'That's all right, Mrs Whasname. You wasn't to know.' Hilda dabbed her bloodshot eyes with a puce-bordered handkerchief. 'I'm being a bit of an old fool.'

There was a clatter as her stick fell to the ground. Charlotte picked it up.

'And who was Katherine?' she asked quietly.

'Little Katherine. She were their daughter, bless her. Lovely little kiddie. Our Joanie didn't have no more.' Hilda lowered her chin into her heaving breast and began to weep again.

'Oh, don't upset yourself,' said Charlotte. 'Would you like to go home now?'

Hilda nodded. 'Where have my Bill got to?'

He had not gone far. He was talking to Jeff Barclay on the front path and was shrewd enough to be making himself pleasant when he realised what Jeff was after. They arranged to meet that afternoon.

Bill returned to Hilda whistling, obviously in a cheerful mood.

'Hey Mother, where's that old clock you go on about?'

At once Hilda rallied. 'Dad always kep' it on the mantel-piece.'

It was not there now.

'Has anyone moved the clock?' said Rosemary. 'Peter?'

'Don't look at me. There was only . . . ' Her look silenced him.

'Come on, that clock!' Bill's tone suggested they were

112

all hiding it from him. 'Worth a bob or two, that clock.'

They searched the house while he stood motionless as a wax figure, waiting, and Hilda repeated over and over that it would be sure to turn up and please not to bother.

In the end Adrian persuaded them to go home, promising he would take it upon himself to find the clock, even if it meant reporting the loss to the police. The mention of this high authority satisfied Bill and he went out to Adrian's car and sat there impatiently waiting for Hilda.

14

The following morning, Rosemary drank a glass of milk, picked up her sketch-pad paints, exchanged her flip-flops for boots and walked out of the house to the gate at one corner of the back garden. Gossamer clung to her face and the air was cool in her nostrils. It was early. She was pleased that she had succeeded in creeping out of bed with no response from Peter and she hoped she had not disturbed Kate.

Once through the gate she mounted the steep bank that divided their garden from the marsh. On top, the path had remained sticky after Friday's rain, where overhanging grass prevented the sun and wind from drying the mud. She was glad of her boots. Her intention was to go along the path until she reached the place where the river turned by the new sluice-gate after it had skirted the wheatfield.

As she walked, Rosemary was brushed by shoulder-high vegetation nodding in the breeze at the side of the path. Great willowherb and ragwort and purple-headed thistles were all too damp to be invaded by the bees that would haunt them later in the day. A wilderness of brambles was studded with pallid blackberry flowers. Webs were strung from stem to stem like moist hammocks.

Where the undergrowth thinned she paused to gaze across the wide marsh. The view was stunning. It was more than she could have hoped for.

Above the line of mist that blurred the horizon the rising sun flooded the sky with a pale yellow glow. The river was a thin band of silver moving fast between two strips of mud which had been uncovered by the retreating sea. They gleamed like pewter, pockmarked by the feet of waders that had probed there earlier for food. The higher ground was overgrown with a sprawling mixture of shadowy green plants in between clumps of sea lavender. Sea purslane, spiked creamy-yellow where the flowers caught the light, clung to the muddy edges of the river, towered over by an occasional bush of shrubby seablite.

Rosemary could see that the colours were changing by the minute as the sun rose. It would be impossible to capture the scene quickly enough if she used paint. All she could do was make a rapid sketch in pencil. Swiftly she worked on a small pad, outlining the bands of light, shading in the darker patches and writing notes to remind herself of the colours. Already the mist seemed to be dissolving and the sky was taking on an apricot tone which was reflecting in the water.

Satisfied at last, she stood for a moment trying to impress the scene upon her memory. Then she closed her sketch-pad and walked to the end of the sea-wall. At this point a new sluice-gate divided the river inland from the part where it changed course to run beside the marsh. The water here ebbed and flowed with the tide twice a day and was dangerous when it started to recede because of the strong current.

Rosemary climbed down from the sea-wall and took the path that followed the river beside the wheatfield.

When she neared the road a solitary duck began to quack. Ben's cottage was not far away and she could see it behind the red Porsche. The car's bright colour was dimmed by the haze. Gradually the other ducks began an agitated noise as if they were being disturbed. Rosemary stopped. Someone was walking purposefully over the grass and through the gate to Ben's cottage. It was a man. He was too blurred by the mist for Rosemary to recognise him. It wasn't Adrian, who had a key, because this man was taller. He had not hesitated and obviously intended to go to the cottage, even at this early hour.

Rosemary waited to see if he would return. She was confident that she could not be seen as only her head would be visible above the ripening wheat. She continued to walk slowly along the path. The light was brighter now. Suddenly she noticed a movement between the hedges bordering the road that led to Marsh House. Her eyes watched the leaves to see who would emerge from behind them.

Kate, wearing a white sweater that belonged to Emma, came into view. She crossed the grass in front of the cottage cautiously, as if hindered by the ducks, who were quieter now. She looked up at the bedroom window and waved. The sash went up and a man's head appeared.

Rosemary heard her call, 'Will I come in?'

A low voice she recognised at once said, 'You horror! Don't make a sound then.'

Kate slammed the gate against the ducks and ran round to the back door. Before he closed the window, Kenneth Weaver leaned out to sniff the morning air.

After breakfast Rosemary went to Kate's room to change her bed. The girl had not returned so Rosemary had not been able to ask her why she had been to the cottage.

The window was open wide, letting in the smell of honeysuckle from the bush in the garden below. Through the gap in the trees Rosemary could see the water in the old harbour glinting in the sun. All the mist had vanished now. The clatter of their lawn mower drowned all other sounds as it passed under the window, pushed sullenly by Colin.

She removed the clothes tossed on to the sheets and added them to the clothes tossed on to the chair. She supposed it was no worse than when Emma was at home, but somehow her own child's untidiness was more acceptable because the responsibility was partly Rosemary's for not insisting that she put things away. She looked about the room.

On the chest all Emma's absurd little creatures had been pushed to one side. The wooden elephant was flat on its back, the drum uppermost on its round stomach.

Kate's white dress had been flung over her Walkman. Rosemary lifted it from habit, intending to put it on a hanger. Underneath, lying on a pile of romantic paperbacks, she saw

116

a tape of Hungarian dances marked K.W. Before she hung up the dress she examined it. Small white flowers embroidered on the bodice, each with a pearl bead sewn in the centre, soft full sleeves gathered into a beaded cuff, rows of narrow tucks alternating with white threaded ribbon from waist to hem – it was not a cheap dress. Parts were grubby but it was too delicate for Rosemary to offer to wash it.

From the doorway Kate said, 'Do you like my frock then?'

'It's beautiful, Kate. It must have cost quite a bit.'

'Not at all. I got it cheap in the Sunday morning market.'

Silently Rosemary placed the dress on the hanger, shaking out the creases. She'd never seen clothes of that quality in the market. When she turned Kate was standing, feet apart, brushing her hair with long sweeping strokes.

'I see you've got some of Kenneth Weaver's tapes,' said Rosemary.

Kate's green eyes were brilliant as she put the brush down. 'Yes. He lent them to me. Isn't he a gorgeous man!'

'Have you seen him today?' Rosemary tried to sound casual.

'No, he's away. Did you not know that?'

At this blatant lie Rosemary decided not to ask anything more.

'Will you lend me his key?' said Kate. 'I'll take the tapes back and borrow some others. I know he won't mind.'

Rosemary hung the dress on the door. 'Better wait until he comes home.'

'You're right. It would be an intrusion,' said Kate demurely.

From outside came the sound of the lawn mower. Kate went to the window and knelt looking down as it appeared round the corner of the house. Like a naughty child changing the subject she said, 'There's Colin cutting the grass.'

'Are you fond of Colin, Kate?'

'Him?' she said scornfully. 'No chance. He's a yawn.'

'I wouldn't have guessed it down by the harbour.'

'I felt sorry for him, the pathetic eejit, he's so smitten.'

'Perhaps if you encourage him it'll be harder for him in the end.'

'Not at all. What's the harm in a few kisses.' She waved at him through the window. The noise of the lawn mower stopped.

'Don't lead him on, Kate,' said Rosemary. 'He's very strong.'

Kate laughed. 'You sound like my mama.'

'Sorry. I didn't mean to nag.'

'It's great you're concerned for me.'

Under the window Colin shouted, 'Kate. Kate, my darling, come down.'

Rosemary was shocked at his imploring voice.

'Will you be finishing the grass first. Then maybe.'

'No. Come on down.'

She blew him a kiss. 'Finish that grass, my lad.'

As she rose from her knees she whined, 'I wish Kenneth would come home.'

Rosemary hesitated. Now was a chance to ask again about this morning. The opportunity was lost when Kate said. 'I'd never go off like she does and leave him. Not for one day. It's her own fault if he's falling in love with me.'

'Oh, Kate, what nonsense.'

'I'm sure of it.' Kate pulled the decrepit holdall from under the bed and took out what Rosemary thought was a tight roll of banknotes. 'Maybe I'll go to the Sunday market on the bike.'

On Emma's bicycle, in Emma's white sweater. Rosemary said nothing as she knew her daughter would not object if she were there. She was generous with her possessions.

'Aren't you going to wait for Colin?'

'No I am not. I thought you'd be glad.' Her mouth widened into a grin. 'Tell him I have a sudden powerful headache. I'll creep away so that he won't see me.'

Along the telephone wire the swallows perched in a row like commas. Below them Dilly smiled at the ducks as she walked across the bridge. Blondie was a hump of feathers standing on one webbed foot, head turned so that her beak slotted in between two wings. She unfolded herself and followed Dilly.

In one hand Dilly carried a pot of white paint and in the other a paintbrush wrapped in a plastic bag, for although the brush was dry now, as she had pointed out to Adrian Petherbridge, it would not be when she returned. She also held a carving knife as the shears were too heavy and anyway, they were blunt.

Half an hour ago Adrian had brought the paint and the boards which he had leaned against the wall of the bungalow near the seat he was determined to repair. He did not begin work as it was Sunday, but he loosened the paint-lid when Dilly asked and lent her his new brush on condition that she washed it thoroughly after use in the special blue liquid from a bottle he gave her. He had gasped and removed the carving knife she held in her hand. Dilly picked it up again when he went into the garden to deal with a clump of marguerites that was tumbling in a white cascade over the grass.

As she walked along the road Dilly nodded to a stranger who dismounted from his bicycle to watch her pass. She was oblivious of the fact that she presented an odd spectacle, holding paint-tin, brush and carving knife, with ducks streaming behind her like rats following the Pied Piper.

Around the small wooden notice that Adrian had erected, which read SLOW DUCKS, the weeds had grown tall, obscuring the faded letters. Dilly leaned over and hacked clumsily away. Alexanders and nettles toppled. She stung her hand and her back began to ache. When she was sure that the notice would be visible from the road she repainted the words using little dabbing strokes. In a tight circle the ducks waddled around her heels while blobs of white fell on to the slaughtered plants.

Painfully Dilly straightened, calling to Blondie, 'Look what I've done for you, lovely.'

The paintbrush was left forgotten on the verge for Adrian to retrieve the following day, its bristles as hard as wire. Back at the bungalow Dilly noticed the marguerites lashed upright into an untidy mop. Many of the flowers had been crushed in the centre. She called sharply for Adrian but it was Rosemary who answered from the path.

'It was Mr Petherbridge I wanted,' said Dilly, almost fretfully.

'I saw him walking up the road.'

'Just look at my poor flowers. If they could scream we'd be deafened.'

'Oh, dear.'

Adrian had dragged the stems into a bundle and bound them neatly with string.

'That man must have everything nice and tidy.' Dilly brandished the carving knife. 'I shall free them.'

In the end it was Rosemary who did so. The marguerites flopped to the ground in a shower of loose petals.

'They need a good drink, mind,' said Dilly. After the watering-can had been filled and emptied by Rosemary they sat in the garden on two folding chairs.

'I told Mr Petherbridge I'm quite content to use these,' said Dilly. 'They're very comfortable.'

'Does he disagree?'

'He wants me to sit over by there, on that seat when he's repaired it.'

'So that's what the wood's for.'

'I'm not sure that I shall be bullied into using it. Have you time for a quick game of Scrabble, dear?'

Rosemary would have happily obliged if she had not promised to call on Charlotte.

'Kenneth Weaver is a dab hand at it,' said Dilly. 'Seven-letter words, that's what he's good at.'

'I think he may be home now,' said Rosemary, hoping that Dilly had seen him.

Immediately Dilly rose stiffly to her feet. 'I'll give him a ring.'

She went indoors mumbling. Rosemary felt mean because she had made the old lady do something that she herself did not want to do. A few minutes later Dilly called from the verandah that Kenneth was not in. She placed two bunioned feet together on each step as she came down.

'Are you sure he's back?' she said. 'Did you speak to him?'

'No. Perhaps I was wrong. I'm certain he'll contact you when he is.'

'Yes.' Dilly went to smell a full-blown rose. 'There's lovely. The reds are best for scent.'

Rosemary agreed and then, trying to sound casual, she said, 'Dilly. Once you suggested to me ... well ... that Ben's death wasn't an accident.'

'Did I, dear?'

'When we were discussing rats. You said he never went out in the dark.'

'Perfectly true. You don't have another number for Kenneth by any chance?'

'Sorry.' Rosemary would not be deflected. 'Have you any particular reason for believing that Ben was pushed into the river that night?'

Dilly spat on a finger and rubbed at a nettle-sting on the back of her speckled hand. The gaze from her intelligent eyes was wary.

'You remind me of Miss Marple, dear. Such searching questions. Is there any point in pursuing it?'

'I'm not just being inquisitive. I'm not going to shout it from the house-tops. But what if someone else is in danger?'

'How very dramatic! I shouldn't think so.'

'Well, let's assume that Ben *was* pushed. Have you any idea who would do such a thing? A harmless old man like that.'

'There would be reasons, I imagine.'

'You sound so sure.'

Dilly answered briskly, 'Let's just say *he* told me, shall we.'

'You don't mean Ben. He knew someone had a grudge against him?'

'Oh no. Not Ben.'

'Who then?'

Dilly smiled. 'Fair play now. You can't expect me to betray a confidence, lovely.'

Adrian came rattling through the gate with a final load of boards in his wheelbarrow before he went home to change for church. If he noticed the marguerites he didn't remark on them.

After visiting Charlotte, Rosemary walked back along her drive. In front of the lodge the laurels were growing absurdly high, the shine of their leathery leaves clouded by dust. She must ask Peter to clip them back before they completely obscured the living-room window. The gate was closed and Kenneth's car was not in its usual place. Had she made a mistake? Was it really Kenneth she had seen that morning? Could it have been Colin or even Jeff? No, it was impossible, Kenneth's voice was unmistakable. He must have returned but now it seemed he had gone again.

Kate had lied, which was not unusual. More to the point, was Kenneth the 'he' Dilly had talked about?

In her handbag Rosemary carried the key to the lodge. Did she have the audacity to have a quick look round to see if she could discover any signs that Kenneth had been back? If he appeared she could make the excuse that she was checking to see that everything was all right in what was, after all, her own property.

She let herself into the hall feeling so like an intruder she nearly retreated in shame. She called Kenneth's name and listened and called again. There was no reply. Apart from a clock ticking ponderously somewhere downstairs the lodge seemed to be protesting silently at her presence. She passed a display of photographs hanging in the hall and went upstairs. In the bathroom the basin was unspotted, with no tell-tale drips. She examined the plug. It was not wet but it could have dried anyway. The soap was hard as a rock and the tank in the airing cupboard was cold.

Through the doorway of the larger bedroom she saw a blue and white shirt flung on the bed. A pair of trainers lay on the floor as though they had been abandoned by

Tosca after a game. The red digits on a clock-radio shone out from a bedside table next to a miniature score of a Beethoven piano concerto and a book describing walks in North Norfolk. She thought it was the one Peter was intending to buy. As Rosemary bent to look, her hand brushed it sideways. Slowly, with great care, she placed it back in its original position, rubbing at the table to hide the dustless strip. She was behaving like a criminal determined to leave no evidence. A trapped fly buzzing at the window startled her. She realised how jumpy she had become.

She went down the creaking stairs into the kitchen. She found she was tiptoeing about. At first glance no one had been there either. A red washing-up bowl was upended on the draining-board. She could see no empty tins or milk-bottles. A dry, crumpled tea towel hung from a bar on the wall.

In one corner of the room, Rosemary noticed a scarlet pedal-bin. She lifted the lid and removed a small empty carton of Longlife apple juice. It could have been there for a long time. Underneath, a triangular plastic container, that had once held a sandwich, crackled a little. She pulled it out and read the label: 'Prawn and mayonnaise. Eat on day of purchase.' Yesterday's date was printed on it. So it *was* Kenneth at Ben's cottage that morning.

In the living room the ivy cast lacy shadows on the window-ledge. The lid of the piano was down, the top protected by a fringed Spanish shawl on which stood two haphazard piles of music. Rosemary saw the antique music-stand with its candles. For a moment she forgot her unease. It was enchanting. She would have enjoyed owning that for no useful purpose, just as a thing of beauty. The room. was far too crowded. The massive three-piece suite, the record-player, chairs and various small tables and a desk were all pushed too close together to make room for the piano. Despite its clutter the room had a feeling of warmth where books were read and music was played. A painting in a style she immediately recognised hung on the wall above the desk. Rosemary squeezed round an armchair to examine it. A Lowry! How exciting to possess an original.

What interesting tenants she had. The wife was a concert pianist and Kenneth, what was he? A writer, a freelance journalist perhaps. Someone who worked at home as well as away.

It really was most unlikely that he was involved in anything sinister. She had become obsessed with an idea that could be perfectly well explained. She would feel ridiculous when she discovered the truth. The door of Ben's cottage must have been left unlocked or Kenneth could have borrowed the key from someone. Perhaps he wanted to buy the place. It would be put up for sale as Hilda could never live there with those stairs.

Just because Dilly had said, 'He told me,' it was absurd of Rosemary to jump to conclusions. She felt relieved as well as stupid. As soon as Kenneth returned she would ask him in for a drink.

She became conscious of a noisy ticking behind her. There was a large oak clock on the mantelpiece. Its case was skilfully carved in scrolls and leaves and the black hands pointed to Roman numerals on a gold face. It was Ben's clock. Kenneth had not taken it from the cottage that morning because it had disappeared before then. So he had visited Ben's cottage on a previous occasion.

Peter ignored the wasp hovering over a bowl of raspberries on the kitchen table. He had blocked the way to the sink by pulling out the washing machine because it had developed a fault. The top had been removed and his eyes were an inch away from the tangle of coloured wires as he tried to discover why it remained locked in one cycle.

His greeting to Rosemary was, 'These modern machines are more complicated than you think.'

'Thanks for picking the raspberries,' she said.

'That's about the last. Any chance of some jam, Rosey?'

'If I've got enough sugar.' She would have preferred to have frozen them as it was simpler. 'Is Kate back?'

'I haven't seen her.'

'Do you know who I saw her with this morning?'

'No. Tell me.'

'Kenneth.'

Peter rattled his screwdriver against a red wire. 'Oh yes. Is he back?'

'I saw him in Ben's cottage.'

'Good.' Peter was being vague.

'In *Ben's* cottage. Peter, could you stop that and listen to me for one minute?'

'I heard. Ben's cottage.'

'*In* Ben's cottage.'

'I didn't know Kenneth was around. I expect it was Adrian. He's got a key.'

'No. It was Kenneth. That gorgeous voice is unmistakable.'

'Is it!' Peter did not look up. 'Did he speak to you then?'

'No. But it was him.'

'Rosey! Do you want me to repair this machine or not!' He tapped a metal disc. 'I wonder if that's the trouble.'

'Please!'

Peter straightened. 'Go on then.'

'Kenneth was in Ben's cottage,' said Rosemary. 'He spoke to Kate through the window. There's no sign of him at the lodge now, but he's been there.'

'Well, I see no problem. All you've got to do is ask Kate.'

'I have and she said Kenneth isn't back yet.'

'I expect she misunderstood the question if he is.'

Rosemary became angry with frustration. She raised her voice. 'Peter, Kenneth's got Ben's clock.'

'I can't believe that.'

'He *has*. You come and see.'

'I'm not snooping. How can you be sure it's Ben's clock? I expect it's a similar one.'

Rosemary could see that she was getting nowhere.

'All right. You ask Kate when she comes in. About Kenneth this morning.'

'If you want me to. Darling, your imagination is working

overtime these days. Kenneth stealing Ben's clock, breaking into Ben's cottage, although we know he's away. And as for Kate having a torrid affair with me . . . '

'I never said that, Peter.'

'Sorry. Only joking.'

The front-door bell rang. It was Adrian dressed in a dark suit appropriate for his role as sidesman at the morning service. His expression suggested that he was the bearer of earth-shattering news but flickered into one of alarm when he saw the washing machine in bits. Broken-down machinery terrified him.

In his hand he held a copy of the *Sunday Times*, folded into a fat square with one item outlined in red Biro.

'What about Kenneth Weaver, then!' Adrian was being pompous. 'We have a celebrity in our midst.'

'Is he here?' asked Peter.

'No, no. He's in the big city.' Adrian flapped the newspaper with the back of his hand and thrust it at Rosemary. 'Read it, read it. The Barbican tonight. Kenneth Weaver playing Brahms' Piano Concerto Number Two. Seven-thirty.'

Rosemary read it carefully.

'Fantastic!' said Peter. 'We got the idea his wife was the pianist. Didn't we, Rosey?'

'Oh no,' interrupted Adrian. 'I knew he was the one who played.'

Rosemary felt more perplexed than surprised. Kenneth had always said the piano belonged to his wife. Was it so absurd to imagine that she was the pianist? Peter would say she had jumped to conclusions again.

Outside the back door she heard a bicycle being flung down, followed by a whirr of spinning pedals. Kate came in, both arms enfolding a giant teddy bear covered in hideous purple fur with a thin orange ribbon around its neck.

'What have you got there?' chuckled Peter.

'Isn't he a fine fellow,' said Kate, planting a kiss on its ear. 'There he was sitting on this shelf imploring me to buy him. And how could I refuse!'

'You carried it home on your bicycle?' said Adrian.

'Yes and why not! Under one arm,' she added untruthfully, for Adrian's benefit.

'You must have a lot of money to waste on junk, young lady!' he said.

'Junk! Not at all. He's a real personality.' She hugged the bear and put her mouth to its ear. 'Aren't you, eh?'

'And where do you find all this money?' said Adrian.

Rosemary and Peter were appalled at the question.

'It's mine, of course. Every penny of it,' Kate said sweetly. 'You'll not be thinking I stole it?'

Peter interrupted. 'Have you seen Kenneth Weaver this morning, Kate love?'

'No. He's away.'

'Of course he is.' Adrian was delighted to produce the paper again.

15

When Dilly came home from morning service she decided to make her bed. It was unusual for her to do so before the afternoon – often she left it until later. The sheets and blankets were dragged across the double bed, enclosing hairpins and balls of Elastoplast that had peeled away from her corns during the night. She pulled up the bedspread and eiderdown of matching slippery pink fabric, oblivious of the crooked angle at which they fell.

Dilly felt tired. She often did, although she would never allow herself a proper rest in the bedroom because that wasted time and was only for the elderly. All she needed was a cat-nap in an easy chair to revive her.

Humming 'And the glory, the glory of the Lord', a remembered anthem from her childhood, she poured out a small glass of South African sherry and took it to the verandah where she flopped heavily on to the Victorian chair. She would have another go at the crossword later. Leaning back with her eyes closed she tried to subdue the busy thoughts that crowded her brain. She was just beginning to feel the muzziness behind the eyes that precedes sleep when her name was called. She heaved herself up and saw Rosemary peering through the front door, looking apologetic.

'What, back so soon, dear?'

Rosemary held up a bag of sultana buns. 'I thought you might like these.' She knew that Dilly would realise they were only an excuse for her visit.

'I was nearly asleep but never mind.'

'I thought you might be interested to hear that Kenneth is the pianist.'

'Oh, someone told me it was his wife.'

'Yes, I did. But it's Kenneth. I mean professionally. In fact he's performing at the Barbican tonight.'

'There's nice, dear.' Dilly seemed unimpressed. 'I'm not surprised, he's such a talented man.'

Across the lane they heard a burst of laughter from the Barclays' garden.

'Someone's happy,' said Dilly.

'Yes. They must be pleased that Ben's cottage might be on the market.'

'I expect Mr Petherbridge has it all in hand,' said Dilly.

'He's been very good. Taking things on as he has. I suppose Hilda will be the sole benefactor. Not leaving a will makes it all the more complicated.'

'Oh, but there *is* a will, dear!' Absent-mindedly Dilly snapped off a dead geranium head.

'No. Ben told me quite recently that he hadn't left one.'

'Well, he must have changed his mind then. My friend Elsie and I witnessed it, see. You'd better come in and I'll tell you the tale.'

Rosemary put the buns down and sat on the verandah half-stifled by the hot air and the aroma of geraniums.

'I think I've been a bit foolish.' Dilly dropped into a chair, legs akimbo. She noticed her untouched sherry and took a sip. 'How naughty of me not to have mentioned it before, although I must say in my defence that one hesitates to tell Mr Petherbridge anything because he's inclined to know already.'

'We haven't found a will in the cottage in any obvious place,' said Rosemary. 'Admittedly we still have some more cleaning and sorting to do.'

'Oh what a nuisance.'

'Tell me exactly what happened, Dilly.'

'Well, Ben called on a Saturday afternoon, the day of the Barclays' party it was, I remember now, when my friend Elsie was here. He was in quite an excited state, clutching a piece of paper. It was his will, folded so that we could not see what he had written, of course it was no business of ours, a very

129

scrappy document, the back of an old envelope I think. Fair play now, one wouldn't expect Ben to have writing paper. I offered him a sheet but he said it was quite all right as it was.' She took a further sip of sherry. 'There, and I haven't offered you a glass, lovely. How rude of me!'

Rosemary shook her head impatiently.

'After Elsie and I witnessed his signature – it was very fortunate she was here, she's brought me a library book she knew was on my list, *Clinging to the Wreckage*, have you read it, dear? – she had to rush away to the shops because some of them close early on Saturday, see.'

Rosemary nodded. 'And what happened to the will?'

'Well, I asked Ben what he intended to do with it. I found shouting to him quite a strain, you know.'

'I suspect he heard more than he would admit to.'

'He said, "I'll put it on the mantelshelf. They'll find it when I'm gone." I kept repeating, "A copy, why not put a copy there and send the signed will to my solicitor?" But he was adamant. "No, missus, I won't."' Dilly shook her head, releasing a flurry of white hairs from their pins. 'Quite rude he was, mind, but that was only his way. He called the solicitors "chaps like black treacle, all over the place". His exact words, dear.'

Rosemary chuckled.

Egged on, Dilly continued, ' "I wouldn't trust them with a farthing bit," he said. The will's not on the mantelpiece, lovely?'

'I'm pretty sure it isn't.'

'Oh, what a pity. I suppose he could have put it anywhere. Have you tried pockets?'

'We'll make quite sure we try everywhere,' said Rosemary.

Vicky was lying in a bikini, arms spread out, soaking up the warmth of the sun like an open-winged bird. She raised her head from the padded recliner.

'Listen,' she said.

Jeff looked up from his copy of *Which Car*. 'Can't hear a thing.'

'That's just the point, darling. No disgusting cough, no shuffling feet or threatening mutterings. It's so peaceful.'

'Good.'

'Everything comes to her who waits.' She closed her eyes behind her sunglasses and leaned back, stretching her long legs which were still a resplendent bronze after a recent holiday on the Costa Brava.

'Yes, darling. All I've got to do now is sort out that pathetic Bill character,' said Jeff.

'That'll be a doddle.'

'I took him for a ride yesterday.' Jeff took a gulp of gin and tonic. 'He was a bit startled at the speed. All he kept saying was, "Mr Thingy say I might get a better offer." That Adrian ought to have his interfering mania seen to.'

'Don't underestimate Adrian Petherbridge, Jeff.'

'I can cope with him. No problem.' He unscrewed the top of the gin bottle. 'Can I top you up, love?'

'I'm all right, thanks.'

He refilled his own glass and flicked over a page of luxury car prices. 'Be terrific, won't it? It's what you wanted.'

Vicky smiled. 'I must say I'm looking forward to that view from the front bedroom. The sea and the sun rising. We could have the bed near the window.'

'You know me. Always prepared to try something new.' He leaned forward to slide up the top of her bikini. 'Like me to ravish you?'

'Certainly not.' She thrust his hand away and reached for a white shirt on the ground. 'Honestly, Jeff, where you get all your energy from I don't know.'

'Please yourself. Plenty of other women are lusting after my body.'

'You're just crude. And big-headed with it. Why don't you go for that swim you were talking about?'

'Could do, I suppose. Won't you come?'

'No, you go. I feel a bit tired.' She fastened the three centre buttons on her shirt. 'I'll get the lunch ready for when you come back.'

'I might ask Charlotte then.'

'All right. Only keep your hands away from her bikini-top, darling. She's a bit of a handful.' Vicky tried to hide a grin, pleased with her unintentional wit.

'Miaow and purr!' Jeff laughed and she joined in.

Someone was walking over the gravel drive and Kate appeared round the corner of the house.

'I heard the noise,' she said. 'So I knew it was no use knocking.'

'Kate. Come along in,' said Jeff. 'I'm just going for a swim and you're the very person to come with me.'

Kate said she couldn't swim and anyway she hadn't a costume.

'Then I'll teach you. And Vicky has dozens of swimsuits. She'll fix you up.'

'No problem,' said Vicky, tartly. 'I've got one far too large for me that you can have for keeps.'

'Well then, I'll accept,' said Kate, apparently oblivious of the innuendo. Before Vicky could go indoors, Kate held out a small brown packet. 'I bought this for you in the market.'

Slowly Vicky unwrapped a soapy-looking plastic troll with hefty legs and sulphur-coloured hair.

'Isn't he grand!' said Kate. 'He stands all by himself.'

The troll was lowered by its hair so that it balanced two broad feet on the table.

'My goodness, so it does,' said Vicky. 'But why me?'

'He's a friend for that doll in the kitchen with no clothes. Will I give her a scrub for you some time?'

'I prefer her dirty.' Vicky swung the troll by its hair.

'Perhaps we should keep them apart,' said Jeff. 'They might produce unacceptable offspring.'

Kate's laugh shook her long hair. Vicky dropped the troll from a height on to the table and went into the house.

'I've bought myself a great bear,' said Kate. 'I couldn't resist him. And now I'm broke.'

'Well, swims are free,' said Jeff.

Soon Vicky came out holding a black one-piece swimsuit and a towel.

'Off we go then,' said Jeff.

'In your gorgeous red car?' said Kate.

'In my gorgeous red car. I'll just get my things.'

'And are you taking Charlotte?' inquired Vicky.

'Charlotte! I expect she's busy getting lunch.'

The bird reserve was separated into two areas of water, divided by a long earth bank, with a large hide standing in the centre. On the seaward side the brackish marsh had been created to provide a feeding ground of mud and salt-water for the wading birds. The freshwater marsh was bordered inland by an extensive bed of dense reed. Sluices controlled the water-levels.

Colin sat on the grass facing the reeds where the bearded tits sometimes came. On several occasions he had seen a small flock perform acrobatics there as they clung to the tall stalks. Today they remained hidden. The noise of the incessant harsh calls of the black-headed gulls obliterated all other sounds.

A small crowd of bird-watchers blocked the path as they watched marsh harriers sitting on the branches of dead trees in the distance. Colin forgot them as his mind became full of Kate. In between bouts of misery he was overwhelmed with happiness. Often he found himself sitting idle for long periods at a time as he allowed the image of her to wash over him. He recalled the smell of her hair when he buried his face in it, the teasing expression in her green eyes when she was not looking at him but knew he was looking at her, the tingling of his skin when his hand reached out to touch her.

She had promised him everything when the opportunity arose. Already she had refused him in the dunes, even when they were there in the dark, because, she said, how could they enjoy such an experience when someone might come along at any moment? And, she said, never in his house because Charlotte would be sure to find out and not understand.

Promises! She was always promising so much and giving so little. His mood swung sharply to despair. A sick feeling churned his stomach when he remembered she had gone off that morning without him. He would never cut the old bat's grass again. She had told him Kate was very sorry but something unexpected had turned up and she would be in touch. He ought to have stopped mowing the moment he saw Kate through the window. He could think of no reason why she should abandon him for good but the fear was always there.

In the distance he saw a girl with long pale hair coming along the path. She was accompanied by a tall man. It was nearly a minute before he could be sure it was not Kate. He stood with his heart pounding and pushed through the bird-watching group. It was crazy to come here on a Sunday when the reserve was full of amateurs, who arrived in cars and coaches. One stupid woman had even brought her dog.

He turned on to the path that led to the large hide which had been designed so that it looked out in two directions. Inside, the backs of a tight row of silent bird-watchers sat before him. They were gazing through the narrow horizontal windows, together with a guide who commented from time to time on the more unusual birds.

'There's a heron being dive-bombed by gulls.'

'Where?' chorused the group.

The guide's voice was monotonous, with no inflexion as he described at great length the heron's position. Impatiently Colin went into the second part of the hide in which were displayed posters of birds to be seen on the reserve, all faded to a uniform shade of blue.

He swung first one leg and then the other over the bench seat. Some of the wooden shutters had been replaced by horizontal panes of glass that could be raised or lowered to make viewing more comfortable in the wind. They were heavy, with frames of thick wood. Carefully he lifted one, using both hands to bear the weight. When it was raised a strong metal hook on the wall held the shutter in an upright position. Slowly he fastened the hook.

Outside the grass grew nearly as high as the window. He

rested his elbows on the narrow ledge and focused his binoculars. Two mute swans drifting nearby turned glistening orange beaks as they became aware of him. Chased away by its tormentors, the heron flew past, its legs held straight behind like arrows.

Colin moved to look across the brackish marsh at avocets sweeping the shallow water with their bills for food.

He heard the door open behind him as the crowd who had been watching the marsh harriers filed into the hide. They raised shutters and began to share telescopes and information. Ill-tempered, Colin went home to a Sunday lunch of roast beef, boiled in a bag, frozen peas and potato crisps followed by rum and raisin ice-cream. Charlotte always said that Colin never had to wait long or eat dried-up food as his meal could be prepared in no time and ice-cream was his favourite pudding.

PART FIVE

16

'Kenneth's back.' Peter fastened his briefcase before he left for work on Monday morning. 'I heard the car.'

Rosemary finished buttering a piece of wholemeal toast. 'What time?'

'About half past one.'

There that part of the conversation came to a halt as Kenneth was still a subject to be avoided.

'It's Charlotte's birthday today,' said Rosemary, brightly.

'Oh, will you be seeing her?'

'Yes. I've got a card and a small present.'

'Good. Wish her many happy returns for me.'

'I will.'

'Well, I'll be off, Rosey.' Peter hesitated. 'Have you seen Kate this morning?'

'No. Should I have? She goes off early sometimes. Why?'

'Oh, no reason. Look, would you like me to ask her how long she intends staying?'

'Yes,' said Rosemary. 'Please.'

'Right. See you this evening, then.' He picked up his car keys and left.

An hour later Rosemary stood in Charlotte's back garden holding the birthday card and a small watercolour painting of the old harbour that she had framed herself. Charlotte had admired it before it was finished and Rosemary was anxious to see her reaction when she unwrapped the completed picture.

While Rosemary waited at the French windows, Mr Puss darted in a straight line across the grass to her. The cat wove

139

figures-of-eight around her bare legs, purring rapturously. She bent to stroke the hard round head.

'She's out, so no amount of cupboard love will get you indoors.'

The cat rolled on to its back and started to clean the fur on its stomach with swift rasping strokes from a pink tongue, as though its life depended on it.

Rosemary left the card propped against the step and took the present home.

The bedroom door was open a crack. Before Rosemary knocked she could feel the stillness that seems to vibrate from an empty room when the owner has gone. She knew Kate was not there.

The room had been returned to Emma again and yet it was not Emma's, for she would never have left it so tidy. The patchwork quilt was straight and unwrinkled, with her old bear placed in the centre. On the chest, where Kate's Walkman had once stood, Emma's ludicrous little animals were arranged like toy soldiers in battle formation, led by the elephant and his drum. The contents of the bookcase were uniformly upright and the overflow had been piled evenly on top. The poster of Klimt's lovers had been replaced by another of a kitten in a slipper some time ago and the fact that it was still there, Rosemary suspected, was more an omission by Kate than an offering to Emma.

Rosemary looked for a note but none had been left. On an impulse she opened the wardrobe door and thrust her hand into the tightly packed clothes. Emma's jingle-jacket had gone.

Vicky closed the wrought-iron gate and came out to the holly-red Porsche carrying the last of the weekend luggage. She cursed at three ducks as they ran towards her, flapping wings for added speed.

Although Jeff had left the house ten minutes before her, there was no sign of him anywhere near the car.

'Jeff!' she called. The mildly disturbed ducks quacked.

Scowling and jingling the coins in the pocket of his city-suit, her husband came hurrying along the road.

'Come on,' she called. 'I thought you didn't want to be too late.'

'I don't. Did you lock up?'

'Of course.'

'And check the automatic lights?'

'I did.'

'Good girl. Off we go then.'

When they were in the car he backed it carefully and then accelerated fast along the road.

'Jeff! Mind the ducks.'

'They'll get out of the way.'

Vicky fastened her seat belt. 'Please keep your speed down, especially on these country roads.'

'We're not in a pram, darling.'

'We don't want to slaughter some pathetic rabbit like we did on the way down.'

'I don't intend to. It mucked up my front wheel.'

Jeff drew in sharply behind Mrs Wolfe, who was taking up more than her fair share of the road, rocking her bicycle from side to side as she laboured up a small incline. Her skirt was rucked well above her plump knees so that she could pedal more freely. As they passed, Vicky waved and raised her eyes to Heaven, silently apologising for Jeff's aggressive road manners.

'What were you doing before we left?' she asked.

'I was talking to that old woman, Adrian Petherbridge,' he said. 'Bloody laugh if the whole thing falls through.'

'What! You don't mean Ben's cottage?'

'He's so pompous he gets up my nose.' Jeff began to ape Adrian. ' "I have taken it upon myself to see that the Wilkinses get the highest offer." Apparently a couple of other guys are showing interest.'

'Jeff, I *will* have that cottage. It's not as if we haven't got the money.'

'I'm not paying over the odds for it, Vick. There are other places along the coast just as good.'

'I don't want any other place along the coast,' said Vicky in a rage. 'I've worked like crazy to make something of ours— '

'All right, all right, don't get your knickers in a twist. This isn't like you. You've been a bit fragile recently. Anything the matter?'

'No. But I will have Ben's cottage. I *will*.'

The force with which Jeff swung round a bend pressed her against the door.

'Jeff, for God's sake. D'you want to kill us both!'

He increased his speed, producing a wind that tossed the flowers and grasses lining the road. The doleful wail of a female singer flooded the car when he switched on Radio One.

That morning Rosemary had intended to drive inland to paint an attractive clump of trees in the centre of a rising meadow, but she was far too worked up to concentrate. She dialled Peter's office number. His voice answered.

'Hello, Peter. It's Rosemary.'

'Oh, Rosey. Hang on.' His muffled words gave instructions to someone.

'Sorry,' she said. 'Is this a difficult time?'

'No, no. You don't often ring me at work. Is it an emergency?'

'Not really. It's just that . . . ' Two of Rosemary's fingers twisted the telephone cord up and down. 'It's Kate. She seems to have gone.'

'And she didn't tell you she was going?'

'No. Emma's room's all tidied up and none of Kate's things are there. And Emma's bike's gone and her jingle-jacket.'

'That coat thing with all the chains?'

'Emma has a passion for that jacket.'

'I'm sure it's only borrowed.' Then Peter said something unexpected. 'I thought this might happen.'

'What! How could you possibly know?'

He hesitated. 'There's something I haven't told you, Rosey. Last night Emma rang from Yugoslavia to tell us she's having a fabulous time.'

142

'And you didn't tell me, Peter!'

'Sorry. Of course I should have. But that wasn't all.'

'Well?'

'She said she'd never met Kate in Dublin or anywhere else.'

After a short pause, Rosemary said, 'I was beginning to guess something like that. Weren't you?'

'To be perfectly honest, no,' said Peter. 'We've entertained Emma's weird friends before enough times. Kate's different, such a sweet kid.'

'I can see now that Betty Tiller fed her with all the information she needed to know,' said Rosemary. 'About Emma going to Dublin. Kate cleverly muddled through the rest. But why was she here?'

'A cheap holiday,' suggested Peter.

'She's not short of money now.'

'True.' Peter sounded rushed. 'Listen, Rosey, Garfield's just come in so I must ring off now and talk to him. Haven't you any idea where Kate might have gone?'

'She's crazy about Kenneth Weaver.'

'Well, try him.'

'Yes. I'll call and find out if he knows anything.'

'Right. Ring me back if he does.'

When Rosemary was walking along the hall she realised that she'd forgotten to ask Peter for more news of Emma.

She opened the front door to see if Kenneth's car was parked in its usual place beside the laurel bushes. It was. So that she would not lose her fast-evaporating courage she went to the lodge door and knocked.

From inside came the scuffling sound of a large dog pounding down the stairs. She heard Kenneth's low voice admonishing the golden retriever in the hall.

'Get your hulking great body out of the way, Tosca.' He opened the door. 'Oh, hello Mrs Lawrence.'

He really was very handsome. Rosemary's timid apology in case she was bothering him made her blush at her own gaucheness.

'Of course you're not. Come along in.'

143

Her entrance was blocked by Tosca.

'Move,' bellowed Kenneth. The dog loped off into the kitchen.

'I'm just making myself a mug of coffee. Will you join me?'

Rosemary accepted as she was ushered into the sitting room. She wouldn't have been surprised to see Kate there, but she was not. A musical score of Liszt Études lay on the piano.

'Did your concert go well?' she asked.

His expression and answer were charmingly modest. 'I think so. I've been rushing about all over the country, mostly in the north and Scotland, so it wasn't worth coming home between concerts. It's good to be back.'

'We got the impression that your wife was the pianist,' said Rosemary, calmed by his warm manner.

'Cat! Good grief, chopsticks is the height of her musical achievement.'

'But isn't it her piano?'

'You've got a point there. She bought it for me when we were married, or exchanged it for a better one because, of course, I had one before.'

'Oh dear! What a stupid assumption to make.'

'Not at all. She's always threatening to take it back if I misbehave. Cat's a photographer. That's why she's away. She's been commissioned to get a book together on Greece.'

'Fantastic! Hot time of the year though.'

'Yes, but good black shadows.' Kenneth thrust his hands into his pockets and smiled at her. 'Actually I'd better come clean about the pianist bit. I didn't bandy it about because all sorts of characters expect free concerts for their favourite charities and it's inclined to snowball. Not that I'm against it but it can be a bit much sometimes.'

Rosemary smiled back. 'That I can believe.'

'I'm surprised you didn't hear me practising.'

'I assumed you were playing a tape or something.'

'I'm afraid it's too repetitive for that sometimes.'

'We hadn't noticed.'

144

'That's a relief anyway. Do sit down.'

As Rosemary lowered herself into one of the armchairs she became aware of the tick from Ben's clock. She dared not look at it. Her sense of unease returned.

'I suppose you don't know where Kate is?'

Kenneth's handsome face took on a look of irritation. 'No, I do not.'

'You haven't seen her this morning?'

Quickly he replied, 'Excuse me. I think the coffee-machine has finished.'

He turned and left the room without closing the door. Rosemary's heart was bumping. It was a mistake to have asked about Kate. His manner had changed so abruptly at the mention of her name that she wished she had the courage to leave. That was impossible because Kenneth would see her pass the kitchen door.

To calm herself down she stood up and pushed by the furniture so that she could examine the Lowry above the desk. The austere people were dark and shadowless, walking on exaggerated feet. Each figure was positioned carefully to make a satisfying pattern in front of buildings painted in warm earthy colours. Rosemary found the picture a delight.

Suddenly, above the tick of the clock, she heard a noise close by. It was a low continuous snarl. Rosemary turned. From behind the settee Tosca's head emerged, her lips drawn back from moist yellow teeth. Bloodshot whites showed below the dark, uplifted eyes.

Rosemary flattened herself against the desk. She saw Kenneth appear, smiling in the doorway as Tosca sprang forward.

Adrian Petherbridge had retrieved the will from Ben's hearth where it had fallen on top of the torn-up electricity bill.

'The number of times I've seen that woman since Ben Pearce died,' shouted Adrian from the bathroom. 'You'd have thought she would have mentioned the will before. We could easily have cleared that room and destroyed it. She's a doddery old fool.'

145

Carol did not hear as her fingernail scratched at a piece of curled cotton embedded in the pile of the carpet or she might have defended Dilly out of sheer perverseness. She was Hoovering through the bungalow, after doing what she referred to as her 'putting away'. This task was non-existent as she always tidied the room before she went to bed each night.

While she rolled the flex round the machine she examined the impeccable room for any object that had the audacity to be in the wrong place. Two carefully aligned Lladro maidens simpered at each other across a burnished wood table, flounced nets, that were looped and ruched into uniform swags, festooned the windows. On the ledge ruby-red roses in a silver bowl had been dragooned into exquisite angles with Oasis and Jeff's chicken wire. They were backlit by the sun so that the petals were transformed to the luminosity of stained glass. A petal fell with a muffled tap. Carol pounced.

She crushed it in her hand, thinking that as Adrian was going to Lynn to see the solicitor she might as well go with him. The jacket she was knitting for herself was nearly finished and she wanted to choose buttons to match. She was anxious to embark on some new project so that she would not feel guilty sitting in front of the television with idle hands while she watched *Dallas* or *Neighbours* or the more enlightening programmes that Adrian enjoyed, like *Panorama*. She had in mind a sweater for him. He preferred cable or plain rib but it was time he got out of his middle-aged rut. Last winter she had met Jeff Barclay in the village wearing an expensive sweater that had silhouettes of dancing women knitted into the front and back. Inspired by this, Carol had discovered in a magazine a garment called 'Bisons', which had eight rows of ginger beasts thundering on small black hooves all around it. The pattern was worked from a chart and did not appear to be too difficult. While she was knitting it she would pretend it was for herself so that Adrian would not object until she had finished. Then, if he adamantly refused to wear it, she would.

146

Five minutes later she came into the bathroom, her hands protected by yellow plastic gloves, to clean the bath. Adrian's face was close enough to the cabinet on the wall for him to mist up the mirror. One finger dragged the side of his mouth back so that he could examine a molar he had hit accidentally with his toothbrush.

'I think it's cracked,' he said, indistinctly.

Folded like a hairpin over the edge of the bath, Carol squirted cleaner and began rubbing at the gleaming surface. 'You should be more careful.'

Adrian's finger tapped the tooth. 'The enamel is remarkably strong.'

'I doubt if you've cracked it then.'

He snapped off a length of dental floss so that he could give each side of the tooth a quick rub. 'I think I'll call in to see the dentist, dear.'

'Why don't you ring him first?'

'An emergency doesn't need an appointment.' He rolled the floss into a ball and tossed it in the bin under the washbasin.

'*Adrian.* I've just emptied that.'

'You can always empty it again, dear. Think yourself lucky you're not married to a gentleman like Bill Wilkins.'

The air filled with steam and noise as Carol turned on the hot tap because she could not think of a suitably caustic reply. After rinsing the bath she turned the water off to say, 'One of the ducks has flown over your wire-netting and made a mess on your path.'

'Vermin!' Before Adrian looked at his tooth again he said, 'By the way, dear, Kenneth Weaver is back. I've been thinking, we must ask him to put on a little concert for your disabled riders.'

'TOSCA, LEAVE.' Kenneth rushed forward to grab the dog's collar. He hauled her backwards. 'How *dare* you!'

The golden retriever became passive and apologetic, cringing into a hump, her tail curling flat between her legs as she slunk into the hall.

Kenneth slammed the door. Rosemary had not moved. Her knuckles were white on her clenched hands as he came forward to lead her to the settee where he sat down beside her.

'She didn't touch you?'

'No.'

'Her bone is under the desk.'

Rosemary turned her head to look. A large marrowbone was grey in the shadows.

'I came in to ask you if you took milk and sugar,' said Kenneth. 'I'm so very sorry about this. Perhaps you'd prefer a brandy.'

'No, black coffee, please,' she said shakily. 'No sugar.'

Later, when she was warming her fingers around the mug, Kenneth said, 'I must come clean about Kate. She was here this morning. But I don't know where she is now.'

He told her that Kate had arrived just as he was getting up and when he had suggested she should come back at a more suitable time, as he was still in his pyjamas, she had refused. Kenneth looked at Rosemary, undecided about whether he should continue.

'Tell me if you would like to,' she said to encourage him.

'She's no relation of yours, is she?'

'Good gracious, no. She turned up one day pretending she was a friend of our daughter. That was a lie although we didn't realise it at the time.'

'Was it now! Well, this morning she threatened to scream for the Petherbridges' benefit as well as yours, so foolishly I let her in. She was wearing this extraordinary jacket affair with daubs of paint and huge glass gems decorating it and chains looped all over the front. Good grief, where she bought the thing I can't imagine.'

'It belongs to our daughter, Emma.'

'Oh dear. Sorry.'

'That's all right. It was Emma's choice not ours.'

Kenneth paused. 'I don't think I should bore you with any more.'

'I'm beyond being shocked by anything Kate does.'

'Well, if you're sure. Suddenly she took off the jacket and underneath she was wearing a skimpy black swimsuit which she proceeded to roll down from the top. She must have been sunbathing starkers because she was as brown as one of Gauguin's bloody Tahitian girls. I started bellowing at her and the little bitch began to taunt me in the most provocative way. She gives the impression of being such an innocent – well, child really. Look, I shouldn't have told you all this. I'm sorry.'

'I'm glad you did. You managed to get rid of her?'

'I told her she was a cheap little tart and disgusted me. While she put on the jacket she sobbed a lot of hysterical rubbish about how much she loved me and how Cat couldn't care for me as she left me alone so much.'

'I think she does believe she's in love with you, if that's any comfort.'

'Not much.' Kenneth gave her a delightful smile. 'I do apologise for using you as a proxy wife. I miss having Cat around to discuss things with. Like some more coffee?'

'I would if it's not too much trouble.'

Rosemary had never considered herself in the role of a sympathiser. That was more in Charlotte's line. Once again she was convinced that Kenneth could explain everything. Any suspicions she had about him were entirely unfounded. Why should the clock on the mantelpiece be Ben's? As Peter said, there must be plenty like it. Of course Kenneth would have a perfectly plausible reason for visiting the old man's cottage. She would ask him about it now and get it settled.

Kenneth came in with two full mugs, saying, 'Do you think Kate's really gone?'

'To be perfectly honest, I don't know.'

'Did I scare her away?'

'I'm sure you didn't. Don't worry anyway. She's quite able to look after herself.' As Rosemary took the mug she said, 'Would you mind telling me something?'

'Of course not. If I can.'

'It's a bit of a cheek really. What were you doing at

149

Ben's cottage yesterday morning? I was out early and saw you with Kate.'

Kenneth grinned. 'I'm sure you were puzzled. It was a last-minute decision to come back. Kate was there because she was out for a walk and spotted me. She'd been a pain before I went away, following me about all the time. I was at the cottage because Ben had given me the key and I'd made a quick dash from London to look for a so-called valuable pendant he'd left on the mantelpiece. Then I had to get back to the Barbican for a morning rehearsal.'

'You knew Ben was dead?'

'Oh, yes. I found out when I rang Dilly. I thought I'd better get hold of the pendant. It was a wasted journey because I couldn't find the thing.'

'A frog pendant?'

'Yes. Ben had said something about diamond eyes.'

'Goodness, no. They're glass. My husband Peter found the pendant and he's looking after it. It's very ugly and not at all valuable.'

'I didn't really believe Ben but I couldn't leave it to chance. We've got a photograph of his wife wearing it.'

'What!' said Rosemary. 'Pol?'

'Is that her name? I think it's hanging in our hall. If not, it's still in the packing case.'

'But why on earth should you have it?' said Rosemary. 'And the pendant? Ben wanted Katherine to have that?'

'That's right,' said Kenneth. 'Katherine is Cat, my wife.'

17

It appeared that both sides of the main street in Hunstanton were lined with parked cars until Charlotte spotted a recently vacated space and backed expertly into it. She had been invited out to lunch by Prue Denton, an old schoolfriend, and because it was her birthday she was going to indulge herself beforehand without the slightest feeling of guilt.

First she visited the bank and then crossed the road to the newsagent where she picked up three thick magazines, more frivolous than informative, and weighed half a pound of walnut fudge from the 'pick and mix' counter. Regretfully, common sense told her that the narrow bands of leather on the sandals in the shoeshop window would cut into her bunion. Half an hour later, carrying a loose black jacket and a pair of outrageously expensive sunglasses, she bought herself a swirl of Italian ice-cream in a cone and sat on a bench overlooking the bus-station. She scanned the waiting queue hoping that no one would recognise her, behaving in a way unbecoming to her new and appalling age.

Her thoughts returned to Kate again. The girl had called that morning when Charlotte was in bed. She had gone down, still in her nightdress. Kate had seemed pleased that Colin was out somewhere, bird-watching. She had been crying, the green of her eyes made more brilliant by the puffy red skin that surrounded them.

'Lovey, what is it?' Charlotte had said.

' 'Tis nothing.'

Charlotte had stepped forward to comfort her.

'No, don't, or I'll start up again.'

'Come on now. Tell me what's upset you.'

Kate lowered her head. 'I've been an eejit. I just came to ask you something – a favour.'

'Yes?'

'If I had nowhere to go could I stay here a while?'

'Of course, lovey. Have you had a row with Rosemary?'

Kate shook her head vehemently.

'What then?'

She seemed reluctant to continue. 'Oh well. T'was Kenneth.'

'Kenneth Weaver?'

'Yes. I called at the lodge to give him a tape I had borrowed. And he tried to— '

'What?'

'You know.'

'Kiss you?'

'Worse. Much worse.' Kate opened her eyes wide.

'No! I can't believe it. Kenneth Weaver!'

'Yes, but it's all right. I managed to get away,' said Kate. 'You can't be blaming him with his wife off abroad all the time.'

'Oh, you poor angel. What an ordeal.' Charlotte hugged her. 'Don't you dare defend the wretched man. Are you sure you're all right?'

'Sure,' said Kate, primly, moving away. 'You'll not be letting me down. About coming here.'

'Of course not, lovey. Come whenever you want. Now, if you like.'

Kate said she was off to visit a friend but she hoped to be back in a few days. She asked something else.

'Will you keep a bit of a secret for me?'

'Of course, Kate.'

The chains on the peach jacket jingled as Kate produced a letter from her pocket.

'This is for Colin to give to Mr Barclay when he's next down.'

'Can't I do it for you?'

'No, wait now. Tell Colin to be sure to give it to him when there's no one else around. It's a secret and very important.'

'Right.' Charlotte took the envelope.

'You see, he's trying to teach me to swim, although I'm sure I'll never learn,' said Kate, confidentially. 'We arranged a date and I'm not sure I can manage it.'

For a moment it crossed Charlotte's mind that the contents of the letter might be different. Did Kate expect Jeff to defend her honour after what had happened? It sounded absurdly dramatic.

Because she was in her nightdress Charlotte did not venture into the garden to wave Kate off. If she had, she would have seen that the basket on Emma's bicycle had a Walkman stuffed into it, protected from damage by the white embroidered dress wrapped around. A holdall, over-full, unzipped and protruding bits of garments, was tied to the back carrier and a purple teddy bear was lashed to it with a belt.

Kate mounted the bicycle and rode unsteadily away.

Five minutes later Charlotte phoned Rosemary, but there was no reply.

The sun melted the ice-cream, sending rivulets down the cone on to Charlotte's hand. Poor little Kate, she thought, she must have been petrified. She remembered the conversation she had overheard between Colin and Kate in the hall. That Kenneth Weaver bloke was a fiend. She could only speculate as to why Kate had come to her and not Rosemary. Why didn't she want to stay at Marsh House any longer? Surely it couldn't be because she wanted to be near Colin. He would be over the moon, anyway. It might give them a chance to establish a strong relationship, once she got over the present sordid little episode.

Charlotte decided she would buy Kate a present, something small and a bit glamorous. A bottle of scent might be appropriate, not too sophisticated, flower-based and with a French name like Fleur de Fleur. That would cheer her up.

After licking the ice-cream from her fingers Charlotte picked up the plastic bags that lay on the bench like coloured balloons and went to the chemist. Finally she bought a shrimp plant from the florist as a thank-you for her birthday lunch and struggled back to the car.

Beside a verge of lofty hogweed and pink sorrel, Dilly walked home from the village shop trundling her basket-on-wheels. She stopped to watch a tiny frog, no larger than her thumb-nail, stretch its long, back legs on the grass as it crawled away from her. She was distressed by the number of frogs squashed paper-thin on the road. It was a pity they could not all survive but a plague of the creatures would be very unpleasant.

In her front garden Blondie was drinking from the man-hole cover of the cesspool. The duck clapped its bill open and shut in the water before lifting its pale head high to swallow.

'How are you, lovely?' said Dilly. 'Let's see if I can find you a nice digestive biscuit.'

Blondie stopped drinking to follow her. Dilly propped the basket on its spike while she searched her handbag for the back-door key. Her nails scraped up fluff and debris from the bottom as she raked about. It did not seem to be there. She turned the handle on the kitchen door and it opened. The key was sticking out of the lock on the other side. She clucked as she bumped the basket over the step and left it in the corner, where it would remain, allowing a small block of coffee ice-cream to soften and ooze through the edges of its cardboard pack.

A shopping-list was half-hidden under a colander of apple peelings. The marmalade and sardines had been forgotten, she discovered. Never mind, she could manage. She had always been forgetful which made her efficient at improvisation.

Outside Blondie was quacking repeatedly like a mechanical toy. Rosemary stepped round the duck so that she could look into the kitchen.

'Hello Dilly.'

'Oh, there you are, dear. Come along in.'

'Good news. Kenneth is home.'

'Oh, that's excellent.'

'He's going to give you a ring when he gets back.'

'I thought you said he was back.'

'From the shops, I mean.'

'I could have done his bit of shopping for him.'

'Yes, well, he's got the car so it's easy for him,' said Rosemary, trying to wind up that part of the conversation. 'I've really come about something else.'

'What's that, lovely?'

'I don't know quite how to put it. You know you said you knew who killed Ben Pearce?'

Dilly frowned. 'I don't think I said that exactly.'

'I'm not asking you to tell me who it was—'

'I only know what I was told, see,' interrupted Dilly.

'I just hope you didn't suspect Kenneth.'

'Kenneth!' Dilly's face appeared to shrink, the lines deepened and her eyes became dull as currants. 'I can't believe that anyone would suspect him. Not Kenneth.'

The telephone rang. Grim-faced, Dilly left to answer it.

'I'll let myself out,' called Rosemary. She took a piece of digestive biscuit from the table and threw it into Blondie's open beak on the way to the garden.

Tiny stones cut into the soles of Rosemary's bare feet as she walked along the shore. A sharp wind had come up that afternoon, blowing the waves in at an angle over the ridges of sand. The sea was iron-grey despite the occasional shafts of sunlight that fell on the water from between the clouds.

Rosemary stopped to look about her. Not the sort of day to paint, she thought. She had forced herself out because it was important she had a large number of paintings so that she could select the best for her exhibition. Also, she wanted to erase Kate from her mind. After the concentration she needed for a painting she found it easier to see traumas in a less emotional way. At least she had no misgivings about Kenneth now.

It seemed a good idea to find a sheltered spot in the dunes as there was no point in ruining her brushes and paint

in the blowing sand. She changed her mind and decided to
be less ambitious. She would draw sea-birds instead. She
took a block of paper and a drawing-pen from her bag and
started sketching the nearest herring gull, that stood among
a crowd of others, all facing the wind. The bird eyed her
warily and walked stiffly away before it ran along the sand,
spreading its wings wide. In a few strokes Rosemary drew
it rising into the air, its pink legs dangling.

When the paper was half-covered with lightning sketches,
she turned her head and in the distance saw Tosca grab at
a stick that had been thrown for her. The great golden dog
charged like a racehorse back to Kenneth. Rosemary went
across the sand to meet them.

'Hi,' he called. 'I thought it was you.'

'I've come out to do a bit of work,' she said. 'But
this breeze has made me wish I'd gone inland.'

'I suppose Kate hasn't turned up?'

'No.'

He pulled a face. 'No ill-effects after Tosca's disgraceful
performance?'

'Not at all.'

'Good. Let me take your bag.'

It wasn't heavy but Rosemary didn't argue. For a while
they walked in silence, obliterating the gulls' footprints in
the sand with their own.

'When will your wife be back?' Rosemary asked.

'Cat? I had an air letter from her this morning. She's still
working flat out but hopes to be home quite soon.'

'Is she travelling around Greece?'

'Yes. She was in Delphi when she wrote.'

Tosca had returned with her stick, which after ritual
growls and tugs she allowed Kenneth to remove from her
mouth. He tossed it high into the sea. The dog hesitated,
looking over the humps of small waves to locate it, before
she thrashed into the water.

'Cruel,' said Rosemary. 'She'll get soaked.'

'She loves it. Anyway she has a choice.' Kenneth stepped
over a clump of sea rocket flowering in the sand. 'I haven't

thanked you for everything you did for Ben. Clearing the house and all the small kindnesses when he was alive.'

'It was nothing. We all helped him. In a small community people rally round.'

'I wish Cat had found him before she did.'

They watched Tosca, the stick clenched between her teeth, as she swam back, head bobbing in the water. At that moment the sun broke through, making the tops of the waves sparkle around her.

'Constable!' said Rosemary. 'The seascape of Brighton at the Tate. Do you know it?'

'No, but I understand what you mean. Constable's flecks of white light.'

Tosca pattered out of the water, gathered herself into a heap and shook. They walked slowly back along the beach until they came to the edge of the dunes where the wind had made a high, sloping wall of sand. At the highest point, hollows curved between the marram grass.

'Let's climb up there,' said Kenneth. 'It's sheltered.'

Their sliding feet vanished under cascades of sand until they reached the top. They sat down, wriggling into comfortable positions out of the wind while Tosca clambered up after them. The golden retriever flopped down, thin and sleek, smelling of wet dog.

'Toshy, you're still in disgrace,' said Kenneth. 'Do you know that?' With a sheepish look Tosca turned her sand-encrusted nose away.

'There's something I should tell you,' said Rosemary.

'Yes?'

'Dilly is convinced Ben didn't die naturally.'

'What!' said Kenneth. 'I can't believe that. It's absolutely ludicrous. There was no query at the inquest. A heart attack followed by drowning. No one else was involved.'

'But suppose drowning came before the heart attack.'

'Nonsense! Who would want to kill an old man like Ben?'

'I don't know. It's just that Dilly thinks someone did. She's no fool, Kenneth.'

'I agree. She's a very bright lady. But the idea is ridiculous. Poor old boy. Isn't it awful, growing old.'

There was nothing more Rosemary could say to convince him. She watched four oystercatchers skim low over the sea towards the bird reserve.

'I'm glad Cat saw Ben,' said Kenneth. 'He was thrilled when they met. She got the Wilkins' address from her father although he hasn't been on speaking terms with them for years. I can understand that. Bill Wilkins was abominably rude, but Cat managed to winkle Ben's address out of her grandmother after a lot of hassle. Cat never gives in. We went to Ben's for the first time on the day of the party, just before she went abroad. She was appalled by his living conditions. She was going to do something for him as soon as she got back, lick his house into some sort of shape. Ben insisted Cat took his clock and promised her the valuable pendant that had belonged to her great-grandmother. He said he was going to search for it and leave it on the mantelpiece. But I've already told you about that.'

'I must get Peter to give it to you,' said Rosemary.

'No hurry. After I'd phoned Dilly I managed to get in touch with Cat. She was really upset. She asked me to send some flowers on her behalf. I would have come myself only I was playing in Edinburgh that day.'

'At least your wife had met Ben.'

'Yes,' said Kenneth. 'Well, I don't know about you but I'm feeling distinctly chilly. And I've got some Prokofiev to work on. I'm afraid you won't get much painting done today.'

'I was only sketching. Will you let me hear you play some time?'

'Of course. And you must show me your pictures. Come on then.'

He stood up and put out his hand to help her to her feet.

Peter drove in and parked the car beside the front door. He carried a large sheet of hardboard into the hall which he was anxious not to buckle because it was to be used to back some of Rosemary's watercolours.

He propped the board against the wall and called her. As there was no reply he went up to Kate's bedroom. The door was open wide and he had to agree with Rosemary, she appeared to have gone. It was a bit high-handed to go off without saying anything but the young were all like that. The fact that Emma hadn't known her didn't worry him overmuch. He guessed Kate would be back with the bicycle and Emma's jacket thing and a plausible explanation some time.

He ambled into the back garden. After the drive home he always found it pleasant to relax in such agreeable surroundings. Above him the wind shooshed gently through the tall trees. If he went on to the sea-wall he might catch a glimpse of Rosemary doing a bit of painting by the old harbour. It was one of her favourite places. Over the reeds he could see a little yellow boat moving into the creek, while two people watched from the road. One might be Rosey but he couldn't be sure. If it was, she'd take twenty minutes to walk home and might be glad of a lift.

He was on his way back to the car, still undecided, when he saw Dilly turn into the drive followed by a pale-feathered, unlikely-looking mallard.

'Oh, there you are, Peter,' she said. 'I'm afraid I haven't come to see you. Is Kenneth in?'

'His car's there so I expect he is.'

'That's a good bit of detective work,' said Dilly. 'Now you stay over by there, Blondie, lovely, in case the big dog comes.'

Peter opened the gate for her and waited while she knocked. The duck waited with him.

'Hello, hello,' he said in a quiet voice he kept for babies and animals. Blondie stayed rigid as a stuffed bird while she regarded him.

'No barking,' called Dilly. 'He's out, see.'

'Come to our house and have a cup of tea,' said Peter. 'Rosemary won't be long. Bring the duck if you like.'

159

'There's kind but I doubt if she'll come,' said Dilly. 'She doesn't get very thirsty. Perhaps I'd better toddle back with her. I don't like her wandering the streets alone.'

'I'm sure she can look after herself.'

'Some of the cars do go very fast round that bend, Peter. I wish they were all as careful as you.'

Peter, who called the overtaking lane on motorways the fast lane and always kept on it, agreed.

'While I'm here,' said Dilly, 'could you give Rosemary a message?'

'Certainly.'

'I've been thinking, as Rosemary keeps asking me, she should know. I'm sure I'm not betraying a confidence. It's only a small part of it, see.'

Peter thought it wise to go along with her and answer as if he understood what she was getting at.

'I'm sure you're not,' he said.

'Just tell her, Colin told me.'

'Is that all?'

'Yes. It's rather like "Barkis is willing". Meaningless if you don't understand. Such a lovely book.'

'Dickens!' said Peter, boldly.

'*David Copperfield*. Rosemary will know what it means. "Colin told me." Have you got that?'

'You don't want me to tell her what Colin told you?'

'No,' said Dilly firmly. 'If she wants to know any more she must ask Colin.'

'Right. I'll tell her.'

Dilly called the duck as if it were a household pet and Peter watched her talk to it, bending her head down to its uplifted beak, as they walked out of the drive. Just before he turned to go back to the house a bicycle flashed by on the road. He went quickly to the entrance but whoever it was had disappeared round the corner out of sight. He was pretty sure it was Kate.

18

The clock on the church tower struck three. It was night and Colin stood on the deserted salt-marsh. He loved this place at night, he felt part of it, alone, yet aware of the invisible wildfowl which he knew were all about him. This was the part of the coast that he could see from his bedroom window. It had been left untouched, unlike the bird reserve which was controlled by man-made banks and sluices.

Early experience had taught him never to walk on the salt-marsh when the tide was coming in. He knew almost instinctively whether it was ebbing or flowing. It fell back now, leaving pools and strips of water palely illuminated by the moonlight. As he walked forward a roosting shelduck rose from the tussocks of grasswort, clattering off in a flash of white.

Colin went on, leaving a line of footprints behind him that quickly filled with gleaming water. Innumerable creeks criss-crossed the marshes. Those that were broad presented no hazard but Colin knew the real danger lay in the barely visible channels where his boots would be sucked into the mud if he trod carelessly. It had happened once and he had had difficulty freeing himself. It was a frightening moment. One boot had to be abandoned waterlogged and he was forced to limp home on a wet freezing foot. Since then he had been wary, always carrying a stick to test the firmness of the ground if he was unsure.

Although he had a sizeable torch squeezed into his pocket, it created dangerous spiky shadows from the carpet of sea purslane that flourished along the side of the creeks. Tonight

Colin's eyes saw well enough in the moonlight. He skirted a patch of tall reeds.

Glancing up at the horizon, where the navy-blue sky met the black sea, he felt exhilarated by the sensation of loneliness. A bright orange flash from a lightship winked at him.

When he reached the firm sand on the shore, he trudged along, watching rays from the hidden sun rise up over the water. Beside him the waves ran up the beach in glittering folds.

One again his thoughts turned to Kate. He could hardly believe his luck. His mother had told him Kate was probably coming to stay although she seemed vague about the exact time. It was unbelievable! So the letter Kate had written to Jeff Barclay meant nothing. Not that he had any intention of delivering it. Anyway, it was lost at the moment and he couldn't remember where he'd left it.

Kate wanted to be with him. He could think of no other reason why she should move from that old bat's house to theirs. Sweet, beautiful, marvellous Kate! How stupid of him not to realise he was being clumsy on the dunes. At first she had been in a teasing mood, sometimes allowing him to kiss her, sometimes not, then for no reason she had gone quiet. She had lowered her head so that her hair covered her face and as he pushed it silkily back she had moaned that she was feeling miserable and needed a bit of comforting. Roughly he had pushed her down into the sand where the marram grass surrounded them like a nest and he had pressed against her and she had wound her arms about his neck as she had never done before.

Suddenly, like a cornered animal she had become violent, punching him roughly and painfully away. Quickly she had got up, scattering sand over him as she tugged down her skirt.

Then she had run across the dunes and along the sea-wall while he shouted threats after her, unable quite to catch up.

None of this was important now because she had chosen

to stay with them. Earlier, he had been unable to sleep, made restless by insuppressible excitement, so that in the end he had dressed and left the house.

Above the debris-strewn tideline the sand was as fine and dry as pepper. It was tossed up from the stamping of his boots as he chanted, 'Kate, Kate,' at every step. Quite soon he tired of this exhausting indulgence. He had reached the spot where a post had been hammered into the dunes, indicating the path that led from the sea end of the bird reserve. He decided to take it.

The light was increasing by the minute, enough for him to see what was about, and the large hide would be deserted. He could make out its dark shape jutting out between the two areas of water.

But first he continued in the direction of the reeds that bordered the freshwater marsh. Even before he was there he could hear the sound he had come for. Ping, ping, ping. A dozen bearded tits hung on the stalks flitting from reed to reed, keeping just ahead of him. The tawny colours that gleamed in the sun were dim now.

The temptation was too great. Dragging the torch from his pocket Colin flashed a beam of light on the small birds. In a blaze of chestnut backs and a purring of wings they flew off. For ten minutes he swung the light slowly across the dense feathery heads of the reeds, but he could see no sign of them.

He retraced his steps. Already the swifts were skimming over the water. Too early for insects, thought Colin, it was hardly worth the effort. Their screams were insignificant compared with the endless rasping calls from the black-headed gulls that smothered the tiny islands, transforming each one into a smokey-coloured mass. Something ought to be done to keep the numbers down. They dominated the bird population on the reserve and stole eggs and chicks and Colin hated them.

He left the door of the hide open. Condensation lay thick on the windows and spots of grey light showed through the tiny knot-holes in the boarded walls. He swung his legs over the bench seat and cautiously raised one of the heavy glass shutters, clasping its thick surround of wood in both hands. He fastened the iron hook attached to the wall to secure it.

He placed his elbows on the ledge and looked through his binoculars, focusing them on a standing cormorant flapping its wings. There was lots of interest to see already as diving ducks plummeted for weed and waders strutted in the mud.

In his ears the harsh calls of the black-headed gulls were deafening. He leaned forward. He did not hear the scrape of metal against metal above him.

The shutter fell. Colin's head was thrust forward, jammed between the ledge and the heavy wooden frame. The thick wiry hair covering his cracked skull became embedded with splinters of glass and blood.

PART SIX

19

Vicky sat in a first-class compartment on the London train to King's Lynn eating an apple. She had not driven up because she wanted to relax, no exertion, no hassle, she had decided. And when she arrived she intended to loll around in the garden in between taking short beneficial walks breathing in the sea air.

Vicky was pregnant. Her body was experiencing sensations it had never felt before. She knew she was right. She knew with absolute certainty that she was expecting a baby. After all the costly tests and the disappointments she had suffered, it had happened naturally. She hadn't been to the doctor, she hadn't even told Jeff and she didn't want him to know yet, the way she was feeling about him at the moment.

It was a row in bed the previous night that had made her decide to escape to the cottage. She couldn't even recall what had sparked it off but it had concluded with words about Kate.

For the first time Vicky had told Jeff about the tortoiseshell and diamanté hairclip. Even now, as she gazed out of the train window at the octagonal lantern on Ely Cathedral, she felt her cheeks pricking with rage. She had been able to cope before but this time Jeff had gone too far.

'I don't remember putting it in my pocket,' he said. 'I must have picked it up after the party.'

These remarks she ignored. She accused him of being so desperate that he wanted to screw that Irish kid from

167

the bogs. An artless child like Kate! It was an outrage!

'Shut up,' Jeff had bellowed. She thought he was going to strike her.

'You monster,' she mouthed, quietly. 'Confine your tarts to old hands like Jessica Doran or Charlotte.'

'Charlotte! You're cracked, girl.'

'Well, it's not for want of trying,' she muttered sulkily, almost believing him.

'And you dare say anything like that about Kate again. She's a terrific kid.'

'Oh, pardon me. You've got me really worried now. Surely you're not getting serious about her.'

'Rubbish! You don't know what you're talking about.'

'Don't give me that old chestnut. I never do, do I?'

Jeff had flung back the duvet. 'You crazy bitch!'

Despite the fact that it was gone two o'clock, he had dressed and run downstairs. She had strained her ears to hear the front door slam, the garage door slide up and the noise from the Porsche fade. She had no idea where he'd gone and she didn't care.

Several hours later, without stopping for breakfast, she had packed an overnight bag and phoned for a taxi to take her to Liverpool Street. A calm note was left on the stairs: 'Gone to the cottage. See you Friday.'

On the train between Downham Market and King's Lynn, Vicky closed her eyes and slowly raised and lowered her chest as she practised deep breathing. She was determined not to work herself into a state.

Wet streaks from Tosca's nose smeared the car window as she looked out on to the narrow road. On his way to Hilda Wilkins's bungalow, Kenneth slowed at a bend made dangerous by the uncut hogweed on the verges. He slowed again to overtake the mechanical flail that was lopping them. During a telephone call that morning, Cat had given him permission to take the frog pendant to her grandmother in Rington. He had not heard that there was a will.

When he left the car at the mean little bungalow, he

thought it was as well that Cat had no conscience about Hilda's living conditions.

'Stay, Toshy.' On the back seat Tosca rested her head on her paws, her eyes uplifted and reproachful.

Kenneth walked up the garden path, hoping Bill was out. Hilda must have been near the scullery door because she opened it at once, wrapped in a heavily starched pinafore of acid-yellow flowers. Opposite the sink Kenneth saw a bicycle propped against a chair. He thought he heard Bill close a door quietly somewhere in the bungalow.

It was apparent at once that Hilda intended the visit to be short as she didn't invite him in. He held out the frog pendant for her to take.

'My wife, Katherine, wanted you to have this. It's the one Mrs Franklin gave your mother.'

The chain fell between her fingers as Hilda examined it. She looked dully at the frog's staring crystal eyes.

'It's the clock I want.' The pendant was a poor substitute. Her eyelids fluttered. 'That one you got at yours.'

Kenneth was mystified. Who had told her where the clock was? Not Rosemary. Surely she wouldn't have done that.

'As soon as my wife comes back from Greece we'll discuss it,' he said. It would be pointless to argue about its ownership now.

'I don't want no discussing.' Hilda's head rocked about as she spoke. She resorted to higher authority. 'Mr Featherbridge. He say he'll see about it.'

'Mrs Wilkins, you might as well know that your father gave the clock to Katherine before he died. He's kept it in the family. Your granddaughter, you see.'

The gleam in Hilda's eye told him that any excuse was unacceptable.

'Well, as I said, we can't do a thing without Cat. She'll be back quite soon. I promise you she won't keep anything she hasn't a right to.'

Hilda lowered her head and shifted one foot to ease the pain in her hip.

'I love that ol' clock,' she whined. 'Sorry I can't ask you in for a cuppa tea.' She gave no reason and seemed distressed by her lack of hospitality.

She waited at the door, listening until he had driven away. Then she hauled herself over the living-room step, calling, 'He have gone now, my little beauty.'

An inner door opened and Kate came through.

Vicky paid the taxi-driver and closed the wrought-iron gate behind her. Inside the cottage, the smell of ancient damp walls pervaded the air. Before she did anything else she opened all the downstairs windows. As she pulled up the kitchen blind she saw an unwashed tumbler in the sink, dark red sediment at the bottom where the dregs of Coca-Cola had dried. Most of the cushions on the settee had a flattened look.

She didn't blame Mrs Wolfe for not tidying up as the woman would not be expecting them until Friday evening. She must call on her before rumours that squatters had taken over the cottage spread round the village. Upstairs the bathroom was strongly perfumed. On the champagne-coloured basin between the gold-plated taps, Vicky's expensive Diorissimo bath-gel was lying on its side with some of its contents oozing out. Her towel hung bunched on the rail. It was slightly damp.

Vicky doubted that Mrs Wolfe had taken advantage of their absence to frolic in perfumed water. It must have been that tearaway daughter, Jackie, she was always on about. What a bloody cheek! What else had she and her boyfriend been up to that left no evidence? Vicky would soon put a stop to all that.

Angrily she locked up and went in search of Mrs Wolfe. Once outside, breathing the clean air while she gazed across to the distant sea, Vicky calmed down. It wasn't necessarily the poor woman's fault. She couldn't be blamed if Jackie had taken the key without asking.

Mrs Wolfe was not a bad little woman even if she was a bit approximate as a cleaning lady. Attending to anything higher than her eye-level she regarded as spring-cleaning but she was trustworthy and willing and a reliable caretaker.

When Mrs Wolfe opened her front door to Vicky, a rush of stew-scented air poured out. In her arms she carried the baby dressed in a too large Baby-Grow that had wrinkled legs and eclipsed his small hands. Vicky's face softened.

'Oh, Mrs Barclay, you're the last person I expected to see,' said Mrs Wolfe. 'You don't usually come till Friday, late. Would you like me to pop up to yours straightaway?'

Vicky said that she wasn't in any hurry and the cleaning could wait.

'That's all right then. And look at me, forgetting my manners. Come along in and take a seat.' In the time it took to walk from the tiny hall to the front room, Mrs Wolfe asked Vicky if she was interested in free-range eggs as Mr Wolfe had just that minute gone to see a mate of his, Freddie Wicks, who had just started keeping hens in his back yard, a bit expensive but plenty of flavour.

Vicky thanked her for the information.

'Let me shift that pile of ironing so you can sit down, Mrs Barclay. Freddie Wicks live by where the telephone box is on the main road, next to Cissie Parker, you know her surely.' She turned to Vicky and whispered confidentially, 'Mr Wolfe say Cissie Parker so short her bum trail on the ground, if you'll excuse me, Mrs Barclay.' She let out a short scream of laughter.

Vicky smiled as she lowered herself on to the cold cushion of a plastic-covered armchair. 'It's your Jackie I've really come to see.'

'She not here, Mrs Barclay. She should by rights be looking after his lordship as she have the day off, but she gone on the bus with ten pounds in her pocket and she'll spend the lot on they fruit machines.'

Right, thought Vicky, and her travels have taken her to my bathroom, but before she could start complaining the telephone rang.

'Oh, please,' she said. 'Let me hold the baby while you answer it.'

Mrs Wolfe hesitated, unsure that he would not cry. Vicky held out her arms to take him. Gently she pushed the baby back on her lap so that his feet rested on her stomach. As she supported his head it felt warm and silky on the palms of her hands. The blue eyes bulged up at her.

Whoever had phoned Mrs Wolfe seemed to be doing most of the talking. Eventually, Vicky heard her replace the receiver and she came into the room white-faced.

'That was Betty Tiller from the shop. She say Colin Franklin have been found dead in one of they bird hides on the reserve.'

'Oh, Mrs Wolfe, how dreadful!'

'Some heavy shutter thing crash down on his head. There's police cars and ambulances all over the reserve car-park, Betty say. That poor Mrs Franklin!'

Rosemary sat in one corner of the sitting room flicking through half a dozen watercolours.

'However do you do those super clouds?' said Kenneth, holding a painting at arms' length.

She got up and came to him. 'Blot them out with tissue while the sky is wet.'

'Really!'

'Yes. Tricks of the trade. I use masking fluid for blocking out creeks and posts and things if I want to sweep a wash right across.' She pointed at a clump of reeds. 'Those have been scratched in with the wrong end of a brush.'

'Good grief!'

'And I flicked murky spots on for stones at the bottom while the paper was wet.' Rosemary laughed. 'I get a bit spattered in the process. But anything goes, unless you're a purist.'

'The result is terrific. I'll have it. How much, please?'

'It's yours, Kenneth. A present. I'm glad you like it.'

He grinned with pleasure as he looked at her. 'Certainly not. I'm not going to demolish your profits.'

'Swop it for a free ticket at one of your concerts?'

He pointed out that there was no comparison as he

172

didn't lose out on the complimentaries. He remained adamant about paying for the watercolour.

'No, I'll frame it and give it to you for Christmas. Charlotte had one for her birthday.'

In the silence that ensued, the apparently snoozing Tosca opened her eyes to look at them.

'How is she?' asked Kenneth.

'Bearing up pretty well. I saw her this morning. An old friend, Prue somebody, had driven over to be with her.'

'What a ghastly accident!'

'Yes. Poor Charlotte,' said Rosemary. 'Let's sit in the garden, shall we? It's nice out there.'

The clicking of Tosca's claws on the brick terrace followed them.

Kenneth leaned back in a chair and closed his eyes. 'D'you know, I'm beginning to have second thoughts about what you said on the beach.'

'What did I say?'

'Ben's death wasn't accidental.'

'Oh, I was making too much of that.'

'Dilly didn't actually say that Colin had killed Ben, did she?'

'No, she said, "Colin told me".'

'That means if he didn't do it he knew who did.'

'I suppose so. Dilly's very upset about Colin. She was fond of him.'

'Excuse me for saying I find that difficult to believe.'

'It's true, though. Charlotte told me. She said Dilly used to coach him at one time. When she gave it up she told him that nearly everyone could read and write but he had this special knowledge about birds that many people would envy. Colin liked that. He often told her about things he'd seen and she was genuinely interested.'

'She would be,' said Kenneth. 'Amazing woman.'

Tosca rolled on to her back, legs splayed and teeth showing, looking foolish. While the dog scraped her tail backwards and forwards across the terrace to attract Kenneth's attention, he leaned over to scratch her stomach.

'And what are your thoughts on our little Irish friend, Toshy?'

'Kate?' said Rosemary.

'Was she having an affair with Colin?'

'Oh no. I don't think so. He worshipped her but she told me she found him a pathetic idiot. Yet for some reason she led him on. I don't think she had any intention of letting him go an inch further than she wanted.'

'It's strange that she allowed even that,' said Kenneth. 'Could he have been blackmailing her?'

'Why?'

'As long as he thought he had a chance he wouldn't give her away.'

'Give away what?'

'Well, that she killed Ben, for example.' Kenneth sat back and gazed at the sky. 'It is possible Colin was out that night and heard or even saw something.'

'But why on earth would Kate want to kill Ben? She'd only just come to the village.'

'I don't know. But just supposing she killed Colin, too. I know no one has suggested he was murdered, but if he was, Kate would have a good reason for doing it if he'd threatened to expose her. She knew his movements, perhaps she'd even arranged to meet him at the hide. She'd only got to sit tight while she waited for him to become engrossed in some bird. Then she could undo the shutter and make a quick getaway on her bike.'

'Emma's bike! I must admit that it seems odd that the shutter fell accidentally. Those hooks fasten pretty securely. But it all sounds a bit impossible to me.'

'Of course. You're right. I was letting my imagination run riot. All the same, I think I'll make my peace with Miss Kate O'Dwyer and see what I can find out.'

On the way back from shopping in Hunstanton, Bill Wilkins crouched in the back of the car dumb with rage. Adrian Petherbridge had just informed them that Ben had made a will leaving everything to his great-granddaughter,

174

Katherine. Adrian had thought that this casual approach might be less of a shock than the news coming direct from the solicitor, or even from Adrian at their bungalow. Gesticulating with the hand that wasn't holding the steering wheel he droned on about formalities and hinted they might get somewhere with a plea of diminished responsibility, but he wasn't hopeful.

Beside him Hilda, with thoughts of her own, was not listening. She couldn't take in that Dad had left everything to the girl who had called for his address not long ago. Someone it was impossible to believe was their Katherine. The little pet who was staying with them now was more like she imagined their granddaughter would be. Bill liked her.

Hilda stared through the crystal-clear windscreen, dreading Bill's impending eruption when they were alone together. Not only had he lost the small car he had set his heart on, told Arty Smith not to let it go to anyone else, but he had been made to look a fool. That mattered far more.

There was no chance now that she would be getting her hip done quickly on the private. And she couldn't ask those people for Mum's clock again. Tears jerked down her cheeks at this final insult.

As he opened the car door to let her out, Adrian told them the piece of news that had been occupying his mind. Colin Franklin was dead. Hilda had to be reminded that he was the son of the lady her mother had worked for. Even then she was too confused to recall who that was.

Adrian returned to the driving seat, offering pompous sympathy and help. Then he went away to offer pompous sympathy and help to Charlotte. Half an hour later, Kate wheeled her bicycle, heavy with her possessions, including the purple teddy bear, out of the scullery to follow the route Adrian had taken to Charlotte's house.

20

The following day, Charlotte rang to say that she was glad of the girl's company and she hoped Rosemary would not be offended if she stayed on. Rosemary said of course not. It didn't seem appropriate at that moment to ask where Kate had been.

Instead she asked, 'How are you, love? Can I do anything for you?'

'Drop in for a chat if you can spare the time,' replied Charlotte, almost brightly. 'The police have just left.'

'I'll come this morning.'

But Rosemary had another call to make first. While she had tried to get to sleep the previous night it occurred to her that Dilly might be in danger, depending on how much Kate thought she knew about the circumstances of Ben's death.

Kenneth's car was not outside the lodge, and as he could be out all day, Rosemary decided to visit Dilly without consulting him. In front of her open kitchen door Blondie rose like a gracious hostess to greet her. Rosemary traced the sound of activity to the sitting room. Dilly was swishing a mop using small brisk movements, redistributing the dust from the wooden surround on to the furniture she had just polished.

'There you are!' She propped the mop against a glass display-cabinet full of porcelain figures elbowing each other for space.

'Have the police been, Dilly?' said Rosemary. 'Asking you questions?'

'About poor Colin, you mean?'

'Yes. They're all round the village. I saw them talking to Mrs Wolfe.'

'No, they haven't yet. I expect they'll be here in a minute. What a terrible thing to happen. I was fond of the boy, you know. Proper nuisance he was sometimes but there was no harm in him. He lived for his birds.'

'Yes, he was strange,' said Rosemary. 'It's a dreadful business. Charlotte's the one I feel really sorry for.'

'Poor girl. Do you think she'll get married again? She's a pretty woman. Has she any men friends, do you know?'

Rosemary wasn't sure but thought Dilly had a point. 'I've brought you half a dozen free-range eggs and a slice of lemon cheese cake.'

She didn't put them down immediately in case they remained forgotten until the next time she called.

'There's kind. Now you're just the person I want to see, lovely. It's a review I read. Wait a minute.' Dilly rummaged through a topply pile of newspapers without success. 'It's not here. Neither is John Mortimer, my library book. Never mind. They'll turn up, they always do. As an expert, why would an artist paint a glossy black square and call it a picture?'

Rosemary knew all the arguments about vibrating colour but expected them to be lost on Dilly as they were on herself, if she had to be truthful. She was let off the hook by Kenneth calling from the hall. He appeared at the sitting room door and produced a paperback of Dorothy Wordsworth's journals from behind his back.

'This is the book I was telling you about, Dilly. Keep it as long as you like.'

'Oh, there's lovely. Now come along in, Kenneth. Entrance us with a little tune.'

She lifted the lid of her upright piano so that he could lean over to try a few experimental phrases. He sat down thoughtfully as if he were playing a concert-grand and let his fingers skim over the tobacco-coloured keys for several minutes. He had not expected the piano to be tuned but he was not prepared for its tinny sound and occasional silent notes.

'Chopin,' he said, stopping abruptly before the piece was complete. Firmly he closed the piano-lid and stood up.

Dilly clapped her hands. He smiled at Rosemary to dispel the embarrassed concern on her face.

'You must hear it on the dreaded Steinway some time,' he murmured for her ears alone.

'Don't say I invited you both this morning and have forgotten!' Dilly disappeared for a topless bottle of flat lemonade and some tumblers.

This enabled Rosemary to tell Kenneth the reason for her visit. He agreed to her suggestion of forewarning Dilly although he did not think she was in any immediate danger so soon after Colin's death, which could easily have been an accident despite what he had said earlier. He was also concerned that a warning, however mild, would alarm Dilly. He was wrong.

'Kate!' she said. 'That child. What could she do?'

'We're not saying she would do anything,' said Rosemary, gently. 'Just be a bit careful. Don't let her into the house when you're alone.'

'Tell me, is she light-fingered, dears? Selling stolen goods could bring in quite an amount of money if one knows where to go,' said Dilly. 'Although I've never tried it myself, mind.'

That would explain a lot, thought Rosemary, surprised that she hadn't thought of that aspect of Kate's borrowing before.

'My kitchen door is usually open. Unless it's snowy or I'm out. Sometimes even then if I forget, see.'

'Try to remember to keep it locked,' said Kenneth.

'I'll do that. Should I keep the windows fastened?'

'Well, use your common sense.'

'Yes. I should hate to lose any of my treasures.' Dilly wiped a moustache of lemonade from her mouth using the back of her hand. 'Did you see that Vicky Barclay is back? She hasn't brought Jeff or that showy motorcar. Perhaps she's planning another party, I enjoyed the last one.'

'Why don't we all go to Castle Acre?' said Kenneth. 'Have a sandwich in a pub afterwards.'

Rosemary couldn't really spare the time as she had eight pictures to frame, but she didn't hesitate in agreeing to the plan. Would they mind waiting while she visited Charlotte first, she asked.

Vicky slammed the front door on her way to the beach. Grieving for Charlotte, although she had not seen her, had exhausted Vicky yesterday, but now, like a storm that had blown itself out, she was calm.

On the grass a circle of mallard ducklings pressed together like a solid furry wheel, their tiny beaks forming the hub. A vigilant mother stopped her preening and waited for Vicky to pass.

She smiled and turned towards the old harbour. At eight o'clock she had been wakened by the telephone. It was Jeff. Immediately she had told him about Colin. When she had finished Jeff asked how Charlotte was taking it.

'I haven't seen her,' said Vicky. 'Do you think I should?'

'Yes or write or something.'

'Wouldn't it be better coming from you?'

'Well, yes, but you're on the spot.'

'Right. I'll try to pop in today.'

Then he had apologised for his irrational behaviour on Monday night and although he was far from humble – he was never humble – she had been won round by his foolish gaiety. A slight twinge of conscience reminded her that she had started it with her accusations about Kate's hairclip. She apologised for being a fish-wife.

He said he had spent the night lying awake in an outrageous tip that called itself a hotel. The breakfast had been something else, bacon, egg, tomato, sausage and mushrooms. He waited for a lecture on calories.

Vicky drew her knees up to her chin under the duvet, groaning as she tried to erase the picture from her mind.

'Anything the matter, Vick?'

She told him about the baby.

He went quiet. 'Are you sure?'

'Certain sure.'

'Has the doctor—'

'Forget doctors, Jeff. I *know*.'

'Well done. You clever little wife. I knew you could do it.'

'Jeff. It's pretty mizz here by myself.'

He said he would drive up tomorrow early. Take a couple of days off. She was to put her feet up and let Mrs Wolfe do everything.

'She's a busy woman, Jeff. She looks after her daughter's baby.'

'Why can't the girl do it herself? This baby of ours will be a genius. Pay her double, treble. That'll stop her being busy.'

Charlotte had eyes that were black-ringed and her usual immaculate hair was uncombed, hanging lankily to her shoulders. They talked about the slight limp that Mr Puss had developed for no apparent reason. Rosemary lifted the cat's paw to examine it. The subject uppermost in both their minds was too sensitive to embark on straightaway.

Charlotte removed the wrapping from a packet of cigarettes and lit one. She said, 'It comes over me in waves. Adrian's been really fantastic. He's taken everything out of my hands. He's in Lynn now seeing to something or the other.'

'I think he enjoys doing it.'

'I know one is supposed to keep busy but all I do is make coffee and light ciggies and sit around. His bits and pieces are all over the place.'

'If I can do anything to help . . . '

'Thanks, lovey.'

Mr Puss appeared at her feet and jumped on to her lap.

'Poor old thing,' crooned Charlotte, running her fingers over the cat's long tail. A flicker of a smile came over her face. 'You don't know what's happening, do you? Stroking is supposed to be therapeutic, isn't it?'

'So I've heard,' said Rosemary. 'Are you sure Kate's not a trial to have around at the moment?'

'No, she's a great comfort. Sympathetic and affectionate. I'd go crazy if she wasn't here. She was up all night playing Colin's tapes because she couldn't sleep, she said. Trying to learn about birdsong, as a sort of link. She's missing Colin badly, she was really fond of him. They might have made a go of it, you know. He was a strange boy, he often went out at night although there wasn't much to see in the dark, I'd have thought. They say he would have died at once, not felt anything. I suppose it wasn't light enough for him to notice he hadn't fastened the shutter properly. He was usually pretty careful about things like that. Funny, you'd have thought I'd have had some kind of sensation when it happened, as a mother, you know. Oh, lovey, stop me burbling on like this. I'm talking rubbish.'

'No, you're not.'

Then Charlotte wanted to tell her about the two plain-clothes men who had called earlier. They had asked a great many questions and had gone upstairs to search Colin's room. His bird tapes were scattered all over the bed which surprised Charlotte because he was methodical about his tapes, keeping them piled in correct number order on a shelf, although the rest of his room was a tip. Then she remembered that Kate had been playing them, but she hadn't mentioned it to the two men.

'Any of your son's diaries or letters that you know of?' the detective, with thinning hair brushed across to hide a balding head, had asked.

Charlotte felt her cheeks burn as she answered, 'No. No, none.'

'Surely he must have had some post. Everyone has post.'

Charlotte had turned her head away. 'Not Colin. He couldn't read or write.'

The man had been gentle and understanding and had apologised again for bothering her and said did she mind if he looked all the same. They had taken away several things belonging to Colin, including the tape-recorder and all the tapes.

Emerging from some half-dream Mr Puss yawned and dug his extended claws into Charlotte's flesh. She thrust the cat to the floor with a curse which set off a fit of coughing. She stubbed out half a cigarette and lit another.

'Kenneth and I have just been to see Dilly,' said Rosemary.

'Don't mention that abominable man to me.'

'Kenneth! He's as nice as they come. And a fantastic pianist.'

'I'm afraid the piano isn't the only thing he applies his hands to.'

'Charlotte! Has he made a pass at you?'

'No. Worse. I could cope. Poor Kate couldn't.'

'What do you mean?'

'He tried to rape her.'

'That's not true, Charlotte.'

'I'm afraid it is. She came here after it happened in a dreadful state. She was a bit reluctant to talk about it but I managed to get it out of her.' Charlotte blew a smoke ring into the air. 'She coped pretty well, poor kid, after what she'd been through.'

'That's appalling!' Rosemary meant the lies. She did not put up a case for Kenneth because it would only anger Charlotte and be unlikely to convince her. 'Where did Kate go before she came here?'

'I don't know,' said Charlotte. 'I forgot to ask.' And she began to talk about Colin again.

Before Vicky sat down on the dunes she looked across the beach to the smooth black rocks exposed by the low tide. Two children with buckets were crouched over a pool like frogs. One stood up and swinging a red bucket ran on thin legs, browner than the sand, to a group of adults sitting in folded chairs.

A wave of maternal love swept over Vicky. She would not loll indolently on the beach while her child went shrimping. She would build sandcastles surrounded by channels for the

182

sea to gush along and play French cricket and Jeff would buy one of those gaudy kites like dragons, which he would let out on a long string until it was a dot of colour tugging in the sky.

There were about eight family parties scattered about; it was worth the trudge along the sea-wall to secure the privacy. Vicky shook out a large beach-towel and lowered it to flatten the marram grass. She lay on her stomach and closed her eyes. After twenty minutes of peace, two children thumped across the sand below her and stopped. Their high voices had boarding-school accents.

'We'll make a slide for the sledge up there, Caroline,' said the boy.

'If we tell Julia she'll want to do it.'

'Then don't.'

'Bags I try it out first.'

'No.'

'*Yes*, Piers.'

'No. It's my sledge.'

This settled they rubbed away at the sand, but whether with hands or spades Vicky could not tell.

Another child arrived.

'I want to help,' she whined, a loser from the start.

'No, Julia, you go somewhere else.' Piers was abrupt and rude. 'We don't want you.'

Vicky had no idea if she had gone or was standing miserably by.

After five minutes more scraping, Caroline said, 'That's getting brilliant!'

'Slow,' said Piers. 'Look here. I've got a better plan. If we climb up and go down on our bums to steamroller the slide it'll be quicker.'

Someone tittered. So Julia was still hanging around.

Vicky heard the noise of softly falling sand get nearer. A smooth cap of brown hair appeared level with her head and Piers's astonished eyes gazed into hers.

'Oh, sorry,' he said, without embarrassment.

'Carry on,' said Vicky. 'I'd love to see your slide when it's finished.'

183

He gave a charming gappy grin that showed the serrated edges of four large teeth. 'You can try it if you like.'

His head vanished as he let himself slither down to Caroline. He repeated the conversation to her although she said she'd heard it.

When the slide was completed, Vicky applauded the children as they took impressive risks for her benefit on the sledge. A plump, limp-haired child, her skin red in patches from careless exposure to the sun, sat ten feet away, jabbing the edge of a spade into a heap of dry seaweed.

Later, unexpectedly tired, Vicky walked back along the sea-wall. 'Please be a Piers and not a Julia,' she said.

Someone was pushing a bicycle over the old sluice-gate. It was Kate. There was no way Vicky could avoid her. Where the path widened the girl waited politely so that Vicky could pass without having to clamber round the bicycle.

'Thanks,' she murmured. As she came close, Kate's mouth stretched into a wide cat-like smile. Vicky's eyes moved with amazement over the white dress. It was entirely unsuitable, far too pretentious for the surroundings, let alone a bicycle. It had been roughly treated. Ribbons were pulled, tucks flattened where the threads had snapped and several parts of the hem were oily from the greasy chain. Grubby was too mild a word to describe the cuffs.

'You're not usually here during the week,' said Kate, in an irritatingly chatty manner.

'No. It was a last-minute decision.'

'Would Mr Barclay be with you?'

'No.'

'He'll be down at the weekend for sure.' When there was no response Kate continued pleasantly, 'You'll be lonely without him.'

Still Vicky refused to be drawn.

'I'm out for a quick breath of fresh air before I get back to my work,' said Kate, mounting her bicycle.

Just before she rode away, Vicky looked down to see the black-painted head of a tiny doll lashed to the handlebars. Wearily she decided she could not face a confrontation.

Kate had barely travelled out of shouting distance before Vicky realised the significance of this discovery. The doll had been on the kitchen dresser quite recently because she remembered seeing it there. The assumption she had made about Jackie Wolfe could be wrong.

That evening, when the sun was moving towards the horizon behind a grey cloud rimmed with a dazzle of apricot light, Kenneth and his dog walked along the road between the creeks. In the harbour the small boats were deserted and motionless. A shelduck flew down, throwing up a spray of water as it skidded to a halt.

Kenneth came to the old sluice-gate and paused, leaning his forearms along the splintering wood. Thank God Cat was coming home at last. He'd had about enough of coping by himself. Serve her right if he had strayed off the straight and narrow. That elfin girl, Perdita, dressed in jumble-sale black gear, who kept turning up at the end of the small, straggling queue of what Cat called, 'fulsome congratulators', in the artistes' room after every London concert, was becoming a bore. An opera student, she'd said she was, fixing worshipping eyes on his face.

'I'm into lieder at the moment,' she'd informed him, after the Barbican concert, '"Gretchen am Spinnrad", that sort of stuff.'

'Interesting piano accompaniment,' he'd remarked, without thinking.

'Yes,' Her eyes told him she'd got the message. 'Finding a rehearsal pianist isn't easy.'

He hoped Cat was behaving herself.

The sun drifted down from behind the cloud, transforming the creek into a patchwork of smooth and rippled gold, even brighter than the sky. Such moments as this refresh the spirit, he'd once heard someone remark, a claim he'd thought at the time both extravagant and sentimental. Now he understood what they meant. If Cat were here she would feel as he did.

He whistled for the invisible Tosca until she came grinning

185

out of some reeds on paws slimy with mud. There did not seem to be anyone about. Kenneth left the old sluice-gate and continued along the sea-wall watching a herd of silky cows grazing in a meadow below. Repeatedly, the golden retriever thundered past him on the path, halting to sniff the grass while she allowed him to overtake, before racing ahead again. On the marsh shining fingers of water were pierced by the dark stalks of reeds that were lit at the top like candles. A sinister place, thought Kenneth, fraught with hidden dangers.

When he reached the point where the sea-wall turned towards the beach he took the opposite route that led to a road a short distance from the village. Because it was rarely used it had become overgrown with vegetation, so dense that only Kenneth's concealed feet could locate the path.

Suddenly, ahead of him, he saw Kate. She was standing, rigid as a figurehead, waist-deep in grass, her hair held back by combs revealing her face illuminated like some angel on a church altarpiece.

Only when she heard Tosca swishing along the path to reach her did she become aware that anyone was near. She turned her head and saw Kenneth. She seemed uncertain what to do. He thought she might walk away to escape from him but instead she watched him come close while she fondled Tosca's ears. She was surprised at his friendly attitude.

'Hi,' he called. 'And where have you been, young lady?'

'Away.' Insolently she flicked an unruly strand of hair over one shoulder.

'So now you're back,' he said. 'Are you staying at Rosemary's?'

'No I am not.'

'Oh, where then?'

'With Charlotte. Though what it has to do with you I have no idea.'

'You're right. Nothing. But I would like to apologise for the other day. I think we both overreacted a bit. Am I forgiven?'

She raised her eyebrows and turned her head away.

'What a terrible tragedy Colin's death is,' he said. 'How is Charlotte?'

'Bad,' she said, almost inaudibly. 'Pacing and talking and smoking most of the night. She doted on that moron.'

'Poor Charlotte. I'm really very sorry.'

Then Kate closed her eyes and although he could see she was making an effort not to cry, silent sobs jerked her head. For a moment he remained where he was. Then he stepped forward to comfort her, placing his arm around her shoulders. Raising the other hand he pulled out the combs, one at a time, allowing her yellow hair to slide through his open fingers. He rested his cheek on her head, while he watched Tosca creep away after some animal trail. Quite soon Kate became still – a stillness that vibrated with sensuality. She lifted her arms to undo his shirt buttons so that she could nuzzle her wet face against his chest and slide her hands along the bare skin until they clasped behind his back. He tilted her head and kissed her with great tenderness before they sank down into the long grass.

PART SEVEN

21

The following morning Kenneth was playing the finale from Schumann's *Carnaval*. On her way to the village shop Rosemary paused at his gate to look across at the small open window, where a great roar of sound burst into the garden. She had no intention of being caught listening but while the music continued and Kenneth was on the piano stool, she was safe.

Out of the corner of her eye she saw Tosca appear from the side of the lodge. The dog padded to the gate wagging her tail. When the music stopped she became skittishly noisy, lifting her head at every bark, going on and on as regular as a metronome.

The window was flung back to its fullest extent and Kenneth pushed his head out bellowing, 'Shut up, Tosca.'

When he saw Rosemary she was sure he frowned.

'Sorry to set Tosca off,' she said. 'I was only having a sneaky listen.'

Immediately Rosemary thought the remark sounded foolish. Kenneth's head disappeared so abruptly that she was unsure if he would come to the door. He did.

'One of my bad days,' he said. 'Nothing will go right.'

'It sounded magnificent!'

'No. I was just letting off steam like a gifted amateur. No control. I won't ask you in. I must get on.'

'That's all right. Forgive me for interrupting.'

He closed the door before she had gone half a dozen steps. She felt the hurt of that frown from the window more than she would have thought possible.

Inside the cottage Kenneth wondered how he could have

been so abrupt with Rosemary. The wretched expression on her face meant that she had gone away imagining it was all her fault, for some reason she would be unable to explain. Yet there was no way he could tell her what had happened when he was with Kate. He must have been mad yesterday evening.

Kenneth returned to the piano and went into the first movement of a Mozart sonata. Cat said that Mozart was like crystal-clear water bubbling in a mountain stream when he played it well. After a minute he slammed down the piano lid and went to the kitchen.

Rosemary had only been home a short time when the telephone rang. It was Kenneth asking her to go to the Plough for a drink that evening.

'Peter won't object?' he said.

'He won't be home till ten. He's working late.'

'Let's go early. About half past six before it gets crowded.'

When she had replaced the receiver, Rosemary went happily back to the studio to finish trimming a mount for a painting.

'Those police fellas have taken all Colin's tapes,' Kate said to Charlotte.

'Yes, I know, lovey. Sorry.'

'Sure, that's no problem. I've heard them all through.'

'All!' said Charlotte. 'You must be an expert on birdsong now.'

Kate looked modest, as though it were true, although the fact was she didn't know the call of an oystercatcher from a thrush. But what she did know was that Colin had lied when he had told her he had recorded the one she had been listening for. She would have recognised the owl and the ducks.

She watched Charlotte light another cigarette.

'Will I get you anything?'

'No thanks, lovey. Just move that ugly brute of a bear so that you can sit down and talk to me. I'm going to miss Colin so terribly. He wasn't easy to live with, he treated the place like a hotel, he was rude and selfish and I used to worry myself sick about him. But you liked him, didn't you, Kate? You obviously found him a caring sort of person.' Her eyes were glistening. 'That's why I'm so glad you're here.'

Kate lowered her head. 'I'm sorry, but I must be off home to Dublin tomorrow.'

'Tomorrow! I don't believe it. Is your air ticket booked?'

'Sure.' For a moment Kate thought Charlotte would ask to see it. 'I've been bothering you long enough.'

'Nonsense. You know that's not true, especially after what I've just said. But how are you getting to the airport?'

'I'll hitch.'

'Certainly you won't hitch, Kate. I'll give you the train fare or even run you to London before I allow you to hitch.'

'I'll not be needing any money, I've got plenty. I prefer to hitch. It's great. I just stand around looking helpless and they stop.'

'We'll see about that. But can't you stay just a few more days? Change the flight. Please!'

'No, I must go. I promised my mother.'

'What am I going to do without you, Kate? This place will be impossible. Promise me you'll come back soon.'

'Maybe, if I can.' Kate grinned as she looked up. 'I'll leave my great bear to keep you company.'

Rosemary sat on one end of the brocade cushion that went the length of a wooden pew in a small room at the Plough Inn. She took a sip of orange juice while she scrutinised an oil-painting of a shipwreck that covered one half of the wall in front of her.

'Did the Victorians think pictures like that were good for the soul?'

Kenneth turned his head to look. 'Very wet and windy. That gold frame's pretty impressive.' He picked up his gin and tonic as he looked appreciatively round at the carriage lamps hanging on the walls.

It was still early in the evening. Through an archway,

rows of light-reflecting bottles and glasses lined the shelves behind the bar, where one middle-aged man flirted quietly with the publican's wife.

'This is peaceful,' he said. 'After all the aggro.'

'Sorry?' said Rosemary, hoping he would explain.

He didn't. 'Well, at least I've made one person happy today.'

'By doing what?'

'I gave that magnificent clock to Hilda Wilkins this afternoon.'

'Oh, that was good of you.'

'Nothing to do with me. Cat gave her orders when she rang. I must admit I did prompt her a bit.'

'That clock meant a lot to Hilda.'

'She grinned like a Hallowe'en pumpkin when I presented it to her. Poor woman! I shouldn't be surprised if Cat forks out for her hip-replacement too.'

'Fantastic!'

A burst of laughter filtered through from the main bar which had an old plough strapped to the ceiling surrounded by various unidentifiable bygones.

Kenneth said, 'I'm a bit concerned about Dilly.'

'Still?'

'Yes. What I'd really like to do is confront Kate to see what her reaction is. I reckon I could get quite a lot out of that girl. It may be cruel but I want to have a go.'

Rosemary was startled at his vehemence.

'Would you mind being there to support me?'

'Of course not, if you want me to.'

'I do. Let's make it soon. I'd like to call on Dilly first though.'

He lifted his glass from the small circular table with a gilded metal base and drained it before he stood up.

'Coming?' he said. 'By the way, Cat will be home next Thursday.'

About half an hour earlier, softly whistling some hymn tune approximately remembered, Dilly went into the kitchen to

194

put an egg on for her tea. She filled the saucepan with water and thought about Kate.

When she saw her come out of Jeff Barclay's cottage last Monday she had been surprised. The girl had smiled impudently as she dropped the keys into her pocket, informing Dilly that Vicky had asked her to water the house-plants while they were in London. Dilly noticed that she seemed to have watered her hair at the same time as it was darkly plastered to her head and there were wet patches on her shoulders.

'She's the biggest liar I've ever met,' Kenneth had said later.

'I've always thought it very restricting to tell the truth, mind,' replied Dilly. 'Although lies do confuse people.'

They had talked about Colin.

'What's your opinion, Dilly?' said Rosemary. 'Did he know who killed Ben?'

'Oh, yes, lovely, he told me he knew. I told Peter to tell you. But he didn't say who.'

Dilly heard spattering and bubbling in the saucepan and looked inside to see a frill of rubbery white that had emerged from a crack in the brown shell. She turned down the heat. Dippy soldiers would be nice with the egg and she would have home-made rhubarb jam spread over any leftover pieces. She loaded two slices of bread into the toaster.

Trailing the unfastened belt of her dress and carrying a tray on which were balanced the egg and an over-full cup of tea, Dilly shuffled to the verandah and landed heavily on the Victorian chair. The saucer brimmed with tea and the egg toppled. She edged the tray on to a nearby bamboo table.

Something pointed jabbed her in the hip. She pressed her hand down the side of the chair and touched a hard corner. It belonged to the library book by John Mortimer that she had been searching for.

A protruding letter acted as a bookmark. It was the one Colin had brought her, the one Kate had given him to pass secretly to Jeff Barclay. Colin had asked Dilly to open it and read it aloud to him but she had refused. His face

195

flushed with jealousy, he had stomped away, slamming the verandah door so that the glass rattled. She never saw him again.

As Kate had seen Jeff since, the contents of the letter were unlikely to be relevant now. Dilly hesitated. This was unforgivable. Against all her principles.

Clumsily her fingers ripped at the envelope. She tugged out a single large sheet and unfolded it. The writing was roundly formed and childlike.

Darling Dada,

I'm sending this in case I can't get through to you at work during the week.

I may be back at Charlotte's by Saturday, but don't you be thinking that her Colin is such a Desperate Terror. I can cope. Did you know that he can't read or write, that is why he is being postman? Isn't that cheeky of me? And I'll not be letting that dragon wife of yours get her hands on this.

First I'm off to old Ben's daughter to charm that divil of a husband of hers. I know he's being difficult about Ben's cottage and he's not above doing something sneaky and I want to make it all REALLY CERTAIN for you. I'll not have us bumping off old fellas if it doesn't get results.

Aren't you glad I came looking for you in the village?

I love you my Dada,

Kate.

The letter concluded with a line of extravagant kisses.

Absent-mindedly Dilly straightened the egg in its cup and with a few brisk taps knocked off the top, while she thought about what she had already worked out for herself.

Vicky Barclay was a very greedy woman and nothing would stand in Jeff's way if he wanted something badly enough. A fatal combination. The final straw must have been Ben's disruptive behaviour during the party. He had gone too far. The Barclays could tolerate him no longer.

Whether Vicky was involved in the actual murder or not, Dilly did not know. Certainly Kate had had something to do with it, as the letter revealed. Despite Kenneth and Rosemary's warning she still could not believe that Kate was any sort of threat to her.

Neither could Dilly explain Colin's death, although she was sure the two murders were related. At first she had thought it unlikely that Jeff would be in the village that night. They only came to the cottage at weekends, staying in London for the rest of the time, and Dilly had not heard of anyone who had seen his showy red motorcar the night Colin was killed. But it could have been too dark and too early and he need not have driven right into the village. The bird reserve was a mile away.

Dilly had decided to make a few inquiries. It was surprising what she could find out if she caught people off-guard with unrelated remarks. Not that she intended to make a habit of it.

The previous day she had met Vicky in Betty Tiller's shop and while they waited to be served they had discussed the merits of decaffeinated coffee.

'Trains,' Dilly had said, purposely introducing a different subject. 'I love trains, especially if some kind friend gives me a lift to the station.'

'No such luck,' Vicky had snapped, tired and fretful after too long a walk on the beach. 'Jeff was away for the night so I was forced to take a taxi both ends.'

So it was possible for Jeff to have killed Colin. Recently Mrs Wolfe had informed a shop crowded with attentive customers that Jeff Barclay had been married twice before and it had crossed Dilly's mind that Kate could be his daughter.

Now she had a letter to prove it, and much more. It appeared that Kate had been a willing accomplice to Ben's murder the first day she met her father.

Dilly lifted the eggshell so that she could scrape the hard white from its cracking base.

'Fair play, Dilys Blodwen Thomas,' she said aloud. 'Not a bad bit of deduction as far as it goes.'

A few minutes later she checked that the verandah was locked, closed the windows and picked up the letter to take it to Kenneth.

Before she reached the kitchen door, which she had inadvertently left open again, she heard the ting of a bell. She stepped outside to see Kate lowering a bicycle on to the path. Its wheels spun lazily to a halt as the girl straightened with a jingle of gold chains from a peach-coloured jacket. A fussy white dress hung below it.

Dilly decided to keep quiet about the revelations in the letter until she had discussed them with Kenneth.

'There's a lovely bicycle,' she said.

'It's Emma's.'

'Oh, she's lent it to you, has she? She's kind like that. Bare feet! You pedal with bare feet. Don't you bruise your toes?'

'No.'

'You be careful, mind. Now what can I do for you?'

'It's the duck I've come about.'

'Which duck would that be, Kate?'

'The one with the goldy feathers.'

'Blondie! Isn't she with the others?'

Kate waved a vague hand. 'I was riding along the sea-wall on the other side of Rosemary's house when I saw her. Injured she is, I think.'

'Injured!' Dilly gave a little gasp. 'Badly?'

'I'm not sure. I tried to get close so I did, but she wouldn't let me near.'

'She'll allow me to, of course,' said Dilly. 'We must go this instant. An injured duck has no chance if she gets near the road. The motorists do drive like fiends round that bend.'

Dilly dragged a small tartan rug from the chest in the hall before they started out together. In silence they walked along the road passing no one. Kenneth did not seem to be at home. In front of the Petherbridges' bungalow their car was barricaded in the garden by chicken wire stretched across the entrance. Outside blue plastic bags were piled, awaiting the dustman. Starlings clicked their beaks on the chimney-tops.

When they reached the corner where the road turned into the main part of the village, Kate indicated the track that went in the opposite direction, by the side of Rosemary's garden.

Dilly glanced round for any sign of her duck. She heard a voice calling, 'Come on, come on,' and looked up hopefully, thinking it might be Blondie safe. A tricycle bearing a plump woman, who enveloped the saddle like a blancmange, rode past accompanied by an elderly puffing dog that was trying to keep up.

She said, 'Hello, Dilly.'

'Hello, Maud. Have you seen my duck, lovely?'

Maud replied, 'No, sorry, dear,' without slackening her speed.

The wide track was mown spasmodically to keep it free from weeds. In Rosemary's garden the holm oaks and Scots pines hung over undisciplined hawthorn hedges, which together formed a high leafy wall. On the other side a meadow, behind a barrier of tall nettles and docks, contained a hen and several feeding rabbits. Dilly scanned the field for her duck.

They climbed to the top of the sea-wall over a strip of grass flattened by walkers. The way down was slow, along a narrow path of soft earth between brambles and great willowherb. The going was rough. Kate took Dilly's arm and helped her to reach the level ground below.

To their left the reeds were over five feet high, extending in a forest of stalks and feathered heads the colour of nutmeg, for a quarter of a mile to the old harbour and stretching in front of them to a strip of moving water. Dilly stopped to look at the fast ebbing river.

'Come now,' said Kate.

Lifting each unsteady foot high, Dilly threaded her way carefully forward. She slithered and skidded across little ridges and furrows invisible under the bending grass. Once she stopped to part the soft heads of the reeds with both hands so that she could peer down between the leaves and stalks. She saw the cold black gleam of water on mud.

'Come along,' said Kate, almost urgently. 'Look, I can see your duck.'

Dilly raised her head. Blondie was sitting motionless on a soft piece of ground where the river met the reeds.

Rosemary and Kenneth stood on the path, contemplating Emma's bicycle. Despite the fact that the kitchen door was wide open, Dilly was out and she was not in the garden. They walked back to Kenneth's car, their eyes searching the road, the wheatfield and the sea-wall that ran behind it, while the ducks fussed around their legs.

It hadn't escaped Rosemary's notice that the holly-red Porsche was parked on the verge.

'The Barclays don't usually come up on a Thursday,' she said. 'Let's call. They just might know where Dilly is.'

Vicky was a long time answering the door. She opened it wearing a thin-strapped satin nightdress.

'Hi,' she said, blinking sleepy eyes that suggested she was only just awake. 'If it's Jeff you're after I think he must have gone out somewhere.'

'Sorry to disturb you.' said Kenneth. 'No, it's Dilly we were wondering about.'

'Isn't she at home?'

'She doesn't appear to be.' Then he added as an after-thought, 'Is Kate here?'

Vicky was scornful. 'That little Irish brat. She is not. I refuse to have her in my house. I don't know what Jeff sees in her. All those hours he spends trying to teach her to swim. She'll never learn in a million years. Sorry to go on, but honestly!'

Then unexpectedly her expression changed and she smiled.

'We overdid the champagne with our lunch. That's why I had a rest. I'm pregnant, you see, and we were celebrating. Look.' She pulled the front door back for them to admire the long-stemmed rosebuds rising from a crystal vase on the table. 'Isn't Jeff an angel!'

They murmured congratulations.

'Tell you what, Jeff has left another sinful bottle chilling in the fridge. Come in and have a glass with me.'

They declined, explaining that they were in a hurry, and left.

As Kenneth closed the wrought-iron gate he suggested they split up. 'I'll drive over the bridge to the village and along the main road looking,' he said. 'You go the other way past your house. I'll knock at Betty Tiller's and meet you at the corner.'

Through the rear window Tosca watched Rosemary as Kenneth dawdled between the mallards in first gear. Hurrying off in the opposite direction Rosemary saw the Petherbridges' car parked in their drive and thought if anyone knew where Dilly was, they would. Rather than waste time discovering how to release the chicken wire, she clambered inelegantly over, scratching her leg.

While she waited impatiently for someone to come to the door, Rosemary admired the massed flowers jostling for space in the narrow beds that flanked the path. The whole garden was drenched with colour.

When Carol appeared she said they hadn't been home long and certainly hadn't passed Dilly or Kate, as she would have noticed. Adrian had gone off for a jog because he had taken it into his head that he wasn't getting enough exercise. She clucked and cast up her eyes and asked, had the dustman been? If so, their plastic bags hadn't been collected and she would have to bring them in before the Wolfes' cat tore out the fishbones.

Plucking some gloves off the table in the hall, she was considerate enough to go into the garden to free one end of the chicken wire, providing a narrow opening which enabled Rosemary to squeeze through. Carol replaced it briskly as if she expected an army of rabbits to appear.

Rosemary saw Kenneth driving towards her. He leaned over to open the door.

'Hop in,' he said. 'Dilly hasn't been near the shop since this morning.'

201

He suggested continuing their search on foot. Parking the car beyond the bridge they found themselves running along the path between the wheatfield and the river, hindered by Tosca who was getting in the way and barking excitedly.

They passed the new sluice-gate and climbed the sea-wall where they were forced to walk in single file beside the thistles and ragwort, carefully pushing away the unruly bramble stems that sprang back after them. They paused to look over the dense thorny bushes to the deep river. The tide had just turned and the current was running fast as the sea retreated. Already a thin line of mud was exposed below the overhanging plants.

Beyond them the salt-marsh was mottled in various shades of green that looked deceptively firm. The silvery foliage of sea purslane marked the edges of hidden creeks and fringed both banks of the river, interspersed with a few sprawling bushes of shrubby seablite.

Far off, a solitary fisherman dug for lugworms. There was no one else in sight.

Suddenly Tosca lifted her head to listen. She heard a distant cry and whined.

Dilly and Kate had been making slow progress. The girl took Dilly's arm again to propel her towards the duck. Without moving its feet it rose up for a second to give a single listless flap of its wings before it settled down.

Crushing clumps of sea aster and glasswort as she flopped to her knees, Dilly patted the feathered head as she talked softly. A small length of cord protruding from under the duck's body caught her attention. She was too busy examining it to notice that Kate was on edge, looking around anxiously.

A few minutes later there was a shout. Kate heard it and looked up to see her father staring down at them over the thickly growing blackberry bushes on the sea-wall.

'Well done, sweetheart,' he called. 'Off you go now.'

Kate turned to face him as she slowly shook her head. She hesitated before she spoke.

'No, Dada.'

'Go now, Kate.'

She began to shout. 'No, I won't, Dada. I'll not have you doing these desperate things. Not any more. Getting me to entice the old fella out was all you asked me to do. There was no need to be harming Colin, divil as he was.' Angrily she clawed her fingers through her hair. 'He didn't record us that night after the party. I've been through all the tapes and there's nothing.'

Dilly listened as she tried to unknot the cord that bound the duck's legs together.

'Shut up, Kate, and go!' shouted Jeff.

'And this old woman, she doesn't know anything,' Kate continued. 'She's an eejit, slobbering over a stupid duck. No one will ever believe a word she says.'

With a sharp twitch, Dilly pulled the cord free. Blondie lifted up on webbed feet, stretching both wings to their fullest extent, and flapped. Kate was too close. One wing hit her leg. There was a sharp sound of cracking stalks as she over-balanced and toppled sideways into the reed-bed. Grabbing at the tough stems with both hands she tried to rise. As she did so, one foot touched the sticky mud and plunged in up to the ankle.

Holding an arm out, Dilly reached as far as she dared. But it was not far enough. Precariously Kate, balanced on a firm mat of flattened reeds, tried desperately to pull herself free. At last the trapped foot came away, accompanied by a loud sucking noise and a jerk that sent her crashing through the reeds, where she landed with the upper part of her body hanging over the river.

Restricted by the white dress wrapped round her legs, she gave a kick in an attempt to wriggle back. She howled as she slipped into the water.

It was shallow near the bank. Slimy mud, soft as butter, began to creep round her. With a tremendous effort she hauled herself upright, only to fall forward, and despite using rapid little paddling strokes she was pulled out of her depth by the rushing current. In despair Dilly watched the jingle-jacket float like a fan behind Kate's sinking head, where it quickly became saturated and was drawn down after her. Dilly saw the colour blend into the mud-clouded water.

Until he heard her cry, Jeff, from his limited vantage point, did not realise Kate was in trouble. He had not been able to teach her to swim. Frantically he ran along the path searching for a way through the interlacing bramble stems. Plunging down at last where two bushes met, his progress was impeded by giant thorns that grabbed his clothes and scratched his face and viciously tore at the skin of his bare arms and legs.

Further along the river Kate rose up spluttering. Her arms flailed, sending clouds of shining droplets into the air. Between fits of coughing she called to her father. As the current swirled her away from him she raised both arms high before she was dragged below the surface.

It took Jeff several minutes to negotiate the brambles. He hauled himself free from the lowest stems, tugging off his shoes as he ran. He paused at the river's edge between bushes of shrubby seablite before he dived far out into the deepest part.

Briefly Kate appeared for the third time, gasping and threshing aimlessly around but calling no more. With a final burst of choking she beat one enfeebled arm on the water and slid out of sight. Horrified, Dilly thought she saw bubbles float up where Kate had disappeared.

Aided by the current, Jeff swam quickly to the spot where he calculated Kate had vanished. He took a deep breath and flung himself under the water. Unsuccessful, he returned without her. He crawled a few strokes before he dived again. It was only after the third attempt that he emerged dragging Kate awkwardly up, clutching her shoulder and the chains of the jingle-jacket. His journey back past the reeds to the bank was exhausting.

There was a bark and Dilly turned to see the golden retriever galloping towards her, followed by Kenneth and Rosemary. Together they leaned over a narrow gap between the sprawling bushes, encouraging Jeff as he kicked against the current, Kate's upraised head between his palms.

When he was near them he reached out to grab a handful of slim, tough branches while the others hauled Kate clumsily out of the water. She lolled like a puppet as she was lowered on to her side. Rosemary left them so that she could run to the house to phone for an ambulance.

Kenneth found the pulse on Kate's neck. They waited. His expression was inscrutable. Gently he turned her on to her back, tilted her chin and pushed aside her hair to uncover her mouth. He hooked out mud and green weed and put his lips on her cold lips and breathed hard into her. Dilly wrapped the tartan rug about her chilled feet.

Beads of crimson blood oozed from Jeff's scratches and trickled down. He was oblivious of the handkerchief Dilly offered him.

Kenneth knelt upright to undo the jingle-jacket and began to push violently on Kate's chest. Crouching beside her, Jeff removed the dripping strands of hair lovingly from her face, uncovering wide green eyes. Enormous pupils stared blankly up at him. He looked at the marbled white and blue-grey colour of her skin and her purple lips. Her head jerked as Kenneth pummelled.

'Leave her,' Jeff said. He was still cuddling her to him when the ambulance men arrived.